STORIES OF OLD CONISBROUGH

Volume 3

Christopher Webster

41

ISBN-13: 978-1539487708
ISBN-10: 1539487709

DEDICATION

To all Conisbroughites, past, present and future.

CONTENTS

INTRODUCTION

This book is the third in a series of story collections about the author's home town, Conisbrough. The stories range from ancient times to the mid-twentieth century, including the experiences of a Conisbrough blacksmith at the battle of Lincoln, a tournament at Pontefract, in which the Sir John Eland, Constable of Conisbrough Castle, wins the prize, and the experiences of a Conisbrough miner during the 'Bag Muck' strike.

1. HANDFASTING AT BURH CONAN

The old chroniclers, Nennius, Monmouth, Wace and Layamon, tell how the first Angle settler, Hengest, had a daughter called Rowena, and how the tyrant ruler of Britain, Vortigern, was so besotted with her that he set aside his wife, Severa, in order to marry her. Of course, the Christian church would not countenance such a marriage, so Vortinger married her by the laws of Woden. This extract from my novel, The Shieldmaiden and the Saint, describes what happened.

I. A WASSAIL

Our fifty ships arrived from Angeln bringing five-hundred warriors and their families. We sailed into the mouth of the Humber, and then along the river Don, until at last we came to Caer Conan. Hengest had been busy in my absence and the hill-fort had been repaired and extended. As the ships were unloaded, Wulfgar, along with other thegns, stood and admired their new home. The view from the river was truly impressive. A huge escarpment rose at a steep angle to what seemed towering heights which were topped by a single palisade, behind which could just be seen the roof of Hengest's high hall. No enemy would ever be so foolish as to attack the fort from that position.

We walked up from the ships until we came to a track that led round the fort to the south and east until it eventually turned north again to the main gate. The land on the south of the fort was a gradual incline, and much more vulnerable, and had therefore been fortified with three palisades, each rising above the other on a steep earth bank. Once again, the warriors were impressed. It was stronger than anything they had seen in Angeln, as Nordic warriors preferred to fight on open ground, and fortifications were therefore less important.

At last we came to the main gate, where the road turned towards the small town of Caer Conan, already being referred to in our language as Coningsburh. It was not an exact translation as none of the Angles knew what Caer Conan meant. With my knowledge of Brythonic, I knew it meant the Fort of Conan, though who Conan was I did not then know.

We had been spotted by the guards on the lookout post, and a large crowd of people were waiting to welcome us. Warriors embraced wives and children whom they had not seen for a year, drengs looked out for nubile daughters whom they might court, tradesmen discussed trade, and farmers the quality of the land. I could not see Hengest in the crowded courtyard, but a guard led the way to the inner ward, and there was Hengest, standing proudly on the steps of his new hall, grinning broadly, and waving at us to hurry towards him. Hrothwyn was too excited to wait. She ran forward, threw her arms around him, and knelt at his feet.

"I'm so happy to see you again!" she said, kissing her hand, and wetting it with her tears.

"And so am I, my lord," said Hildeburh, coming up a

few moments later and throwing her arms around Hengest's neck.

They had much to tell each other, but there were other greetings to be exchanged.

"Welcome, Wulfgar, and your son, too! Welcome Wulf! Thank you for taking care of my family. I'll bet it was not easy."

Wulfgar laughed. "I had rather fight the Frisians again than look after that lot!"

Hrothwyn was too overcome with emotion to notice this remark, but a look of anxiety swept over Wulf's features.

"But here they all are! In one piece, as you see!" Wulfgar continued.

Wulf looked relieved, he had feared that his father was going to relate the sorry tale of their raid, but the conversation moved on quickly.

"And what of Octa?" said Hengest.

"Ah! My lord, he was bitterly disappointed, but he is doing his duty like a good son should."

"I'm glad to hear it," said Hengest. "I don't know what he is so disappointed about. He will be here before long."

"That's what you said last time," replied Wulfgar wryly.

"I forgot the hot blood of these drengs!" laughed Hengest.

"Not just the drengs, my lord. We older men can still give them a run for their money! For myself, I am delighted to have the chance to fight at your side once again!"

Hengest put his hand on his shoulder and shook him firmly. "Thank you, Wulfgar. Old loyalties are never forgotten."

Then he looked round the teeming courtyard, and with a sweep of his hand to encompass it all, said, "But we have much to do. I want you to help me to quarter the new men – and we have a feast to prepare for! Come inside, and we will make a plan..."

But before they could begin they were interrupted by a messenger. "My lord, King Vortigern has arrived!"

Hengest looked towards the main gates, where in the middle of the confusion caused by the throng of his own people, he saw a column of soldiers dressed in the semblance of the armour of Imperial Rome. They looked impressive enough to the Angles, but compared to real Roman legionaries they were a ramshackle lot, their armour, though well-made, often fitting badly, and consisting of ill-matched bits and pieces. Vortigern himself looked like an old vulture as he bent his scrawny neck this way and that as if trying to find his prey in the crowd that thronged to greet him. Though not more than 50, he looked at least 70. His skin was wrinkled and drawn tight across his face adding an unpleasant emphasis to his beak-like nose. He wore an old Roman cavalry officer's parade helmet which was studded with jewels and inlaid with gold, an elaborately carved muscled cuirass, and over that, a thick cloak of imperial purple.

Seeing his guest of honour arriving, Hengest forgot all about the new arrivals for a moment, and started giving orders to his retainers to ensure that the king received the welcome that befitted his status. It was only when they had gone to carry them out that he noticed me. "Harfeax, forgive me, I overlooked you in my greetings."

"No matter, my lord, it is not so long ago that I last saw you."

"True, my old friend. Welcome, nevertheless, and thank you for taking the message."

"It is always a pleasure to serve you, my lord."

"Well, show my family to my private quarters, then find Horsa, and send him to me. We must give King Vortigern a welcome fit for a... fit for a... well, a king, I suppose!"

And with a little laugh at his own joke, Hengest hurried off to the main gate with Wulfgar beside him.

Wulf should have followed, but he wanted to catch a

few word with Hrothwyn, as he realised he would probably not get chance to speak to her again until after the feast.

"Shall I say something tonight?" he whispered.

"Yes," said Hrothwyn, then noticing that Wulf was looking anxiously to right and left like a hunted criminal, added with a light laugh: "Don't worry. I have told my mother, and she approves. She will pretend that she has not noticed us talking. Did you tell your father?"

"Yes," said Wulf, "and he was very serious about it. He says that I must speak to lord Hengest first, then if he approves of the match he will negotiate the details."

Hrothwyn was radiant with happiness. "Wait until the formal part of the feast is over, the speech-making and saga singing, then see if you can find an opportunity to speak to my father alone."

Wulf made a movement towards Hrothwyn, but recollected himself, and said, "I will. I will watch him like a hawk until the moment comes!"

Then, blowing her the kiss that he was not allowed to give, he ran after his father and Hengest.

Hrothwyn dressed with extra special care. Tonight was the night when she would be accepted as Wulf's future wife, and she was dressing for him. Her maid, Mildreth, began to twist her abundant blonde hair into braids in Hrothwyn's usual style, but with a touch of the hand, Hrothwyn stopped her and said, "No, I want to try it like this..." She pointed to a Roman urn which had been intriguing her since she first entered her chamber. It was probably a gift from Vortigern which Hengest had put there in an attempt to decorate her apartment. It was unlike anything she had seen in Angeln. It was finished with a mirror-like glaze that dazzled her, but what she found most interesting was the scene depicted on the urn, which showed Roman lady of fashion pouring wine into her husband's wineglass.

"Look at that hairstyle, Mildreth," she said, pointing to

the urn. "I like the way it is piled high on the head, then falls down in ringlets. Can you do mine like that?"

Mildreth studied the urn doubtfully. "I'll try ma'am," she said, "But you'll need a special comb to hold it, and you don't have one."

"I know, but perhaps we can get one from the village."

So a comb was sent for, and Hrothwyn busied herself in study of the rest of the Roman lady's attire.

"Look at her neckline," she said thoughtfully, "it's so low! And look how thin the material is."

"There's no time to have a new dress made, ma'am," said Mildreth, wishing that the urn had been put somewhere far away where Hrothwyn would never have seen it.

"That's true," said Hrothwyn sadly. "I'll have to do the best with what I've got. Let's look through my chest and see what I brought."

Just then, there was a knock at the door. It was her father. He came in at her invitation and stood looking around awkwardly as if he didn't how to begin. Mildreth, sensing that he wanted to talk to his daughter in private, curtsied and went to see about the comb, leaving them alone in the room. The first thought that came into Hrothwyn's mind was that this was a good chance to prepare her father for what Wulf had to say to him later that night.

While she was thinking about this, Hengest cleared his throat nervously, and began, "I want you to look your best tonight, Hrothwyn."

Her heart leapt within her. Did he know already? Had Hildeburh perhaps told him of her love for Wulf, and suggested that tonight's feast would be a good time to arrange everything?

"And I want you to be especially nice to King Vortigern."

"Of course, father!" she said, somewhat surprised at the request. Surely her father knew that she would do her best to honour such a special guest.

Hengest looked uncomfortable. He grunted, shuffled his feet and looked hard at her, then looked away again. He was obviously struggling to say something. Hrothwyn decided to help him.

"Father, has Wulf…"

"Wulf?" said Hengest, seeming unable to understand the word, his mind being on something else altogether. "What has Wulf got to do with it?"

"Father, we…"

But it was too late, Hengest, having delivered his orders, had nothing else to say, but many more things to attend to. So leaving his daughter anxious and puzzled, he turned on his heels and hurried off to attend to them, congratulating himself on a job well done.

Hengest's new high hall at Coningsburh rang to the sound of rejoicing as hundreds of Anglish thanes celebrated their new home. King Vortigern, magnificent in a toga of imperial purple, sat in state with Hengest at the high table, along with Horsa, Hengest's family and his leading thegns. Next to Vortigern was Ceredic, his most trusted adviser, but there was no sign of his wife and daughter, as he had left them in Caer Ceint.

When all the guests were assembled, Hengest sent Hrothwyn to perform the welcome ceremony. She took the welcome cup to King Vortigern and said, "Lord King, Waes hail!" but Vortigern smiled and shook his head; he still couldn't understand Anglish speech, let alone their strange customs, but I was ready as ever to interpret, and explained her words and what he should do next. King Vortigern thanked me, and drank from the cup, as was the custom, all the while watching every move this fair maiden made. Vortigern had seen nothing like her. Dark-haired Britons tricked out Roman style, he had seen plenty of, but this fair skin and corn-gold hair dazzled him like sunrise after a dark night. He beckoned her closer and added a kiss to the welcome ceremony, though the kiss was warmer and longer than a mere welcome kiss.

Further down the hall, Wulf was watching all this with anguish, as he realised before Hrothwyn did what was going on: King Vortigern was taking a fancy to Hrothwyn, and the fancies of kings can be dangerous – especially where women are concerned!

When Hrothwyn had taken the welcome cup around the hall according to the custom, she returned to the high table, and Vortigern signalled that she was to sit beside him. He called me over, too, so that I could help with translation.

"And what is your name, pretty lady?" he began.

I translated.

"Hrothwyn, my lord."

Vortigern tried to say the name, but stumbled on the 'hr' and the 'th', sounds which do not exist in Latin. "That's a brute of name for such a beautiful woman!" he exclaimed. Then, turning to Caradoc, he said, "Caradoc, we must rename her! What would you call her in your language?"

Caradoc thought for a moment, then replied, "Ronwen, my lord."

Vortigern said the name to himself a few times, weighed it, measured it, then rejected it. "It's nearly right, but a woman so beautiful should have a name with a Latin form. Let me see. What would it sound like if I added a feminine, nominative ending: Ronwena. No, that's not right. What about Rowena? Yes, that's it! Rowena. A beautiful Latin name for a beautiful Angle woman!"

Hrothwyn didn't understand most of what Vortigern said, but she caught the gist of it, and quite liked the sound of her new name. She gave a girlish laugh and repeated it to herself several times: "Rowena, Rowena, Rowena!"

The new name suited her so well that, from that day on, she was always known as Rowena, even by her father and Hildeburh. Indeed the name was so beautiful that it was passed on to future generations of the English-speaking peoples. As for Hrothwyn, she came to associate her old name with her shieldmaiden-self, and her new name with her recently discovered female-self.

Rowena, in obedience to their father's wishes, spent most of the evening at the King's side while I hovered discreetly in the background to help with translation when necessary. She laughed at Vortigern's jokes (though she didn't understand them) and refilled his cup whenever it was empty. It was only when Vortigern slipped his arm round her waist and pulled her towards him for another kiss, that she realised belatedly what was happening. She struggled against him, pushed his arms away, and tried to escape him altogether. But he held her more firmly, and forcibly planted a kiss on her lips.

Then everything seemed to happen at once. Wulf jumped to his feet and tugged at his sword hilt, which luckily was tied by peace bands. He fumbled with the bands, but before he could loose them, his father had pulled him down again and was hissing harsh words into his ear.

At the same time, Rowena's alter-ego, Hrothwyn, had sprung to the rescue of her new female-self, and she had whipped Tyrfing from her belt. Hengest, who had been watching Vortigern's love-making with intense interest, saw this, and immediately grabbed her wrist, twisting it so that she dropped her blade. Then he heaved her to her feet and nodded to his wife, who knew what she must do. She hustled Rowena, still wriggling to get free and fight her corner, into the private quarters for a good talking to.

This all happened so quickly, that anyone who was not watching would have missed it, though now, hearing the sounds of the scuffle, more and more eyes turned with curiosity to the high table. But Hengest was already on his feet calling for a toast to King Vortigern.

"King Vortigern!" everyone roared, jumping to their feet

and raising their drinking horns.

"And to my new home at Coningsburh!"

"Coningsburh!" the people replied.

In those few moments Hengest had drawn everyone's attention from the embarrassing scuffle, even Vortigern's, who probably saw it as no more than a little hiccough in his designs, which he would resume as soon as Rowena returned. Hengest now needed a longer distraction, no doubt to give Hildeburh time to make Rowena see her duty. So he called for me.

"Sing me a new saga," he said, "and call it The Saga of Hengest, for tonight is the peak of my achievement. I have suffered exile, and with nothing but my sword and my loyal thegns, I have sailed across the sea to a strange land, defeated an even stranger people in one great battle, and been given much lands as a reward: Thongcaster, Coningsburh and the whole of Linnaeus, which I will call New Angeln!"

I hesitated. It was bad luck to compose a saga for a man who still lived, for a saga is a cradle-to-the-grave story, and the twists and turns of Wyrd can turn any achievement upside down at the eleventh hour, or as the Havamal puts it: "Count no man happy until the end is known." I tried to reply diplomatically, "No man's story is complete until he returns to the All-Father, and believe me, my Lord, you have even greater deeds to do – let me sing again of your victory over the Picts."

"No! It must be a saga!" insisted Hengest. His voice was still pleasant, but there was an edge to it.

"I can but offer a beginning," I said unhappily.

"Then begin," laughed Hengest.

I struck a chord on my lyre and the hall fell silent. Then, with a prayer to the gods to ward off ill omen, I lost myself in another world, a world of legends and heroes, fate and hard-won fame. Then the words came, woven afresh to ancient formulas, almost as though some poetic spirit possessed me. I sang of Hengest's early struggles in the Frisian feud, the war-keels that had carried him to Britain, the battle with the Picts, and the culmination of his career at Coningsburh. Then with the snap of the final chord, past and present, saga and real life, had merged, because the last words of saga were about this very feast.

The hall resounded as the thegns roared their admiration of Hengest's achievement, and I think, my skill in telling of it, but I was trembling from the strangeness of that last moment. It had been a clever poetic device – to merge literature and real life like that, but it was no way to end a saga. There would be a proper ending one day, I knew it, and I prayed again that it would be a good one.

Just then, Rowena came back into the hall, looking very cowed. Her face looked as though it had been washed with tears, then hastily dried and made up again. I could imagine what Hildeburh had said, and I saw that it had been effective when Rowena returned to her seat beside Vortigern.

Hengest's voice snapped me out of my reverie. He had been impressed by my saga, and thanked me warmly. Then, looking meaningfully at Rowena, he said, "Sing us a love song."

I know that he intended that I should create an atmosphere in which Vortigern's love-making might flourish, but at the risk of incurring my master's wrath, I chose something which I felt was more appropriate: the Song of Wulf and Eadwacer, a song which I had song not long ago in Angeln, but now it had a different resonance:

I am on one island
She is on another
Defended by fens and fierce warriors.
I could brave every danger
But our fates are forked.
Eadwacer, Eadwacer

I am weary with wanting her
My heart is hollow
Hungry for her love.
But our fates are forked.

I heard Rowena stifle a sob and regretted my choice. I had not meant to upset her. But perhaps it was just as well if she took to heart the words of the refrain and realised that, as far as Wulf was concerned, her fate was now taking her in a different direction.

However, I needn't have worried about Hengest's displeasure. Vortigern's suit was prospering, and he seemed well pleased. In fact, Vortigern was so taken with Rowena that, before the evening was out, he asked Hengest if he could have Rowena for his wife. That was just what Hengest had hoped for, and he agreed with obvious delight. This was success beyond anything he had ever dreamed of. Indeed, so great was his happiness, that he quite forgot Vortigern's royal dignity, and slapped him on the back like an old drinking companion. The union of King Vortigern and his daughter meant the union of the two peoples, and that his grandson would one day be King of Britannia, though perhaps by then it might have another name – Angleland.

II. THE RITES OF PAYNIM

Of course, there were problems, many of them. The first was that King Vortigern expected to bed Rowena that very night. This Rowena absolutely refused, saying that she would be married before she surrendered her maidenhead – or would die defending it. For once, Hengest supported her. He knew all too well that many a man's ardour has cooled when he has enjoyed the feast prematurely. Then there was the problem of Severa, Vortigern's existing wife.

Vortigern made light of this, saying that he would get an annulment, though he looked less confident when Ceredic whispered into his ear that it might take years before that could be arranged. Luckily, it was less of a problem for Hengest. Under Danish law, a man could take more than one wife, and the custom was not unknown in Angeln, so he simply proposed that Rowena should be an additional wife, on condition that she was recognised as the chief wife. Vortigern tried to explain that such an arrangement would be against the teaching of his religion. After listening to the wrangling for a while, I thought I could see an easy solution.

"Let Vortigern keep his wife under Christian law, and take Rowena under Woden's law," I suggested.

Both Vortigern and Hengest seized on this as a good solution, and that led them to the next problem, the brideprice. Fortunately, Vortigern, hot with desire, was in a mood to be generous. "I will grant you the sub-kingdom of Ceint," he said. "Lord Garengen has displeased me lately, so I will be glad to depose him."

After a bit more negotiating, and the concession of a wedding as soon as it could possibly be arranged, Vortigern added the gift of Caer Lundem, which is a large and prosperous town on the river Thames.

The wedding took place next day as promised, and in the absence of a godi, I was asked to officiate. It took place in Hengest's high hall, and though it was packed with Angles, very few of Vortigern's followers were there. Apart from his legionaries, he had only brought a dozen duces and tribunes with him, and about half of those had baulked at the thought of their king being wedded to a pagan woman in a pagan rite, with no priest, no mass and no blessing. They felt sure the wrath of God would fall on Vortigern, and though it could cost them their wealth, and perhaps even their lives, they felt they could play no part in it.

Vortigern was so hot with lust for his pagan princess that he didn't even notice their absence, but stood with Ceredic before the high table, along with myself, Hengest, Horsa and Hildeburh.

At last the great door opened and Rowena was led into the hall by her attendants. She was dressed in a new gown made especially for the wedding, and modelled after the Roman fashion. It was a magnificent garment of finely-woven white cloth, low at the front, like the picture on the urn, and trimmed with gold thread. Round her neck was a gleaming golden pendant given to her by Vortigern, and round her arms were bands of gold. The overall effect was thoroughly Roman in style. The only Nordic feature being her wide belt with Tyrfing attached horizontally to the front of it, She looked truly ravishing, and she was only a few minutes away from being a queen – but she couldn't appreciate it; she would have rather married Wulf wearing an old sack and been mistress of his small mead-hall in Angeln.

Her maids escorted her to the high table, and I asked her to stand beside king Vortigern, who was magnificent in quasi-imperial finery. Then I announced that the brideprice and handgeld would be exchanged. The brideprice was the dowry and the handgeld was a small gift given by the bride to the groom.

"Do you have the handgeld as you agreed to have?" I said to Hengest.

"I do," he replied, and gave to Vortigern a wooden model of a white horse. "The real horse is waiting for you outside," he said with a laugh. "A white horse is my emblem, so it will remind you of the link between our families."

Then I turned to Vortigern. "Do you have the brideprice as you agreed to have?"

"I do," Vortigern said, and turning to Hengest, he handed over documents confirming his lordship of Ceint and Caer Lundem.

Then came the most important part of the ceremony; the exchange of oaths, sealed by the exchange of swords. Hengest handed a fine heirloom blade to Vortigern, though I noticed that it was not Battle-Flame – only death could part Hengest from that sword! Vortigern, who had been primed by me before the ceremony, now presented a sword to Hengest; a Roman spatha, a long sword, a little longer than the Nordic broadsword, and even better forged. This was followed by the exchange of rings. Vortigern placed a ring on the third finger of Rowena's right hand saying, "I bind you to me with this ring."

Rowena then placed a ring on Vortigern's talon-like finger with the words, "I bind myself to you with this ring."

Vortigern gave Rowena a bunch keys as she was now his lawful wife, and the keeper of his household. Of course, that bunch of keys was only symbolic. If Vortigern had given Rowena all the keys to every door in every hall he owned, she would have had a wagonload. Finally, I took both their hands in mine and raised them to show everybody that they were man and wife. The half-hearted cheer that was given in response was bad enough, but one voice was heard above the others shouting, "May God curse you, Vortigern, for betraying your country!" The guards at the door marched into the crowd at once, but no-one was caught. Whoever it was must have had a lot of support, because nobody betrayed him.

Vortigern tried to make light of the matter, but it was clear that it had disturbed him. Hengest couldn't care less about it because he had got what he wanted – an alliance with the king of Britannia. If anything, he thought it rather funny, and had to bite his lip to stop himself joking with Horsa about it. As for Rowena, she was too distressed to find herself the wife of a man she didn't love, or even like.

The unsettling interruption was quickly forgotten when everyone went to the tables for the serving of the bridal mead and the bridal banquet. Everyone fell to with a will amid pleasant sounds of talk and laughter. There was a different atmosphere in the hall today because now the womenfolk were present and their light laughter and girlish giggling mixed with the gruff laughter of the men. The young drengs were particularly enjoying themselves because it was rare that they had a chance to see so many young, unmarried maidens at one time, and a feast was a good time to get to know them. Only Wulf looked solemn.

Then I was called upon to sing an epithalamion in honour of the couple – I will not say "happy couple" because one of them was ecstatically happy and the other in the slough of despond. A poem of this kind should begin with a recitation of the honours of the bridegroom, describe the beauty and worth of the bride, and end with wishes for a fruitful marriage and a happy future; but I was somewhat at a loss what to sing about Vortigern. I knew something of his achievements, and they were very great. He had gone from nothing to King of Britannia, or Imperator, as he preferred to be called. He had pulled together the remnants of the legions, recruited mercenaries – my master Hengest and his thegns – and had managed with his help to hold out against the raiding Picts, Scots and northmen. But every achievement seemed to be tainted with evil. He had achieved kingship by murder, and he was now in the process of undermining his success by going against his religion. On top of that there were many stories about his cruelty, arrogance, womanising – and worse; rumours of unspeakable goings-on his daughter, Ardora. Nevertheless, it is true that many, if not most, of the lords we skalds serve are far from being good examples. It is an essential part of our art to find something noble to sing about. After racking my brains for a few minutes, I finally hit on the idea of singing of Magnus Maximus whom I had heard about from a local bard. He was revered amongst the Romano-Britons because he rose from the post of Military Commander of

Britannia to become Emperor of the West. In so doing he brought glory to a distant and despised province, though it is conveniently forgotten that, in his quest for the purple, he stripped Britannia of its legions and left it vulnerable to raiders. There was also a link with Coningsburh that I knew Hengest would find interesting:

> *When Magnus Maximus ruled in Rome*
> *he dreamed one night of a beautiful damsel*
> *in a wonderful, wealthy far-away land.*
> *When he awoke he sent his warriors*
> *all over the world. They found her in Wales,*
> *a chieftain's daughter in Caernarfon.*
> *She was young, she was fair*
> *and had red-gold hair.*
> *and, very important, was still a virgin;*
> *that maid was Helen. She married Maximus*
> *and loved him as much as he loved her.*
> *He rewarded her father with the realm's lordship,*
> *but he seized the throne and threatened to kill him*
> *if he should come to recapture the country.*
> *But the men of Britain led by Conan Meriadoc*
> *removed the usurper and recaptured it for him.*
> *Conan is famous in Coningsburh,*
> *for this was his city — once called Caer Conan,*
> *and now it is Hengest who holds this burh,*
> *given to him by a another great emperor.*
> *So hold your drinking horns high for the toast:*
> *Vortigern, the new Maximus! The virgin*
> *Rowena, the new Helen! — and Hengest,*
> *the new Conan!*

My epithalamion was greeted with loud applause, but only from our own people. Few others could understand it. However, Vortigern nodded his approval. As I ws the singer, I could hardly translate it for him, but he had recognised the names, and knew that I was comparing him to the most famous of Britain's rulers. As for Rowena, if she had been listening, she probably reflected that she would not be "the virgin Rowena" for much longer, and so it proved to be. Vortigern drained his drinking horn, then rose from the table with a significant look at his bride.

III. SHIELDMAIDEN IN THE BEDROOM

At last they were alone! Bliss to Vortigern – bane to Rowena! He barred the door behind him to ensure that his long-anticipated love-feast would not be interrupted and eyed Rowena lasciviously. For her part, she had made up her mind to do her duty, however unpleasant. She was Vortigern's lawful wife now under Woden's law – and for any other law or religion she cared nothing. Under Woden's law it was her duty to surrender her body for her lord's pleasure and to provide him with sons and heirs. She knew that her father wanted that too – an heir who would his grandson and King of Britannia.

Vortigern lumbered towards her, pushed her onto the bed and started to unfasten her robe. His drunken fingers fumbled with the laces, and in a fit of frustration, he tore her gown open. All the while, he was huffing and puffing like a broken-winded horse, and breathing his wine-foul breath all over her. Rowena could not help but remember the tale of Hildeburh's suffering, and resolved that she would not allow the same thing to happen to her. She rolled out of his clumsy grasp and got to her feet in one quick movement.

"My lord," she said, "I am your wife and will do my duty, but there is no need to attack me like a bull in heat! You are spoiling my clothes. Please allow me to undress myself first."

Vortigern got to his feet his face sweating and red with

rage. "How dare you speak to me like that!" he roared. "Do you know who I am?"

In all his fifty-odd years of fornicating with wife, wench and serving-woman, no-one had ever dared to speak to him in that way. But Rowena, typical of her people, cared nothing for status.

"A feeble old man – that's what I see before me. Just a feeble, drunken, old man!"

Vortigern bounded towards her, swinging his arm for a blow. "Why, I'll teach you!" he roared.

But he was no match for a shieldmaiden. Quick as lightening, she had blocked his blow with her left hand while her right had drawn Tyrfing and held its point to his throat in one adroit movement. Vortigern froze in terror.

"I will never let you beat me!" said Rowena sternly, "Once I was a shieldmaiden, and though I have set aside that way of life, I can still best you in any fight!"

"Ha!" scoffed Vortigern, recovering his confidence somewhat. "It is easy to say that with a knife at my throat."

"With or without my seax," she added, throwing it behind her so that Vortigern couldn't get it.

"Now I'll show you!" he roared, and grabbed her gown again. But she unbuckled her waistband, turned around quickly, and the gown came free in his hand. As he looked at it in amazement, she grabbed one end, danced behind him, grabbed the other end, then pulled it up round his throat and started to throttle him. Vortigern's face went purple but he could do nothing to break her hold, however hard he pulled, because she had twisted the material to give her more leverage.

"You are too slow, old man," she taunted.

But Vortigern couldn't reply – he was choking to death. Suddenly, she let go and Vortigern fell forward under the force of his own attempts to pull free. Rowena kicked him on the backside to help him on his way. He fell face down into a spluttering heap on the floor and lay still.

"Now, my lord," said Rowena. "If you promise to be gentle, you may take me — that is, if you still want to."

Vortigern rolled over and looked up at Rowena who stood over him in a posture of victory. Her magnificent blonde mane had escaped from its comb and hung over her shoulders like a golden halo. Her face was flushed with exertion, and her half-exposed bosom heaved deeply. To Vortigern, she was more desirable than ever.

"I promise," he said meekly.

And his promise was well rewarded. Rowena slipped out of her torn shift, pulled up his shirt, straddled him, and lowered that heavenly triangle of blonde down on his urgently waiting manhood. lowered that heavenly triangle of blonde down on his urgently waiting manhood.

2. EXCALIBUR AT ROCHE ABBEY

This story, which is an extract from my novel, Sword of Albion, deals with the history of the sword Excalibur before it came into the hands of King Arthur. The key events of the story are set at Roche Abbey, but I imagine this to be an earlier, Celtic foundation, as the Roche Abbey we know today was founded in 1147.

I

The next day they set off through the north gate of Ratae. At Masgwid's suggestion, they had left their horses in the care of the innkeeper. "The going will get tough, even for mules!" he had warned them. Aurelius bid a sorrowful farewell to his beloved Achilles, and whispered, "I wonder if I will see you again." Then, to make it more likely he said to the landlord. "I value this horse more than..." he was going to say the conventional words, "my life", but he changed it to "your life" with a strong emphasis on "your". To make assurance doubly sure, he gave the landlord a gold solidi. The landlord took it with a trembling hand. It was probably the first he had ever handled.

The mules were loaded and they made their way, leading

them slowly along the semi-ruinous streets towards the north gate. They followed the Via Fossa for a few miles, then turned off to go due north, and as Masgwid had warned, the track was rough and the going was slow. For several miles there were signs of cultivation, and they sometimes saw labourers in the fields, but thereafter the land seem neglected, and there were few signs of human inhabitation. The landscape was undulating, and the fields were broken up by forested hills, some of which came right down to the trackway and almost overwhelmed it.

"I don't like the look of this," said Aurelius. "If good land is neglected, it means there is a risk of raiders. We need to be on our guard. Have your swords ready under your cloaks. I will take the vanguard. Publius, watch our rear. Masgwid and Gruffen, keen a sharp look out to either side."

They marched on slowly, straining their ears for warning sounds, but all they heard was an oppressive silence. The noonday heat seemed to cast a mesmerising stillness over everything. There was no bird song, no animal movements in the hedgerows. All they could hear was the occasional snort of a mule and the sound of their own footsteps. Aurelius walked on in a kind of trance He was trying to keep a look out, but his mind was drifting into a kind of walking sleep. He gave a sudden start when he realised that Publius had left his post in the rear and was walking beside him. Before he could say anything, Publius hissed, "Don't look around, my lord, but we are being followed."

Aurelius was suddenly wide awake, and all his senses were alert. "How many?"

"One man dressed in a black cloak."

Aurelius thought for a moment. "Perhaps he is just another traveller. Well, we will see. Warn the others, and tell them that, when I give a sign, to slow right down. We will see if he catches us up. If he does. All well and good. If not, I want you to hide in the underbrush and catch him when he passes."

At Aurelius' signal the travellers slowed down until they were barely moving, but the man did not catch them up. Aurelius gave another signal, and Publius disappeared into the underbrush while the group returned to its normal pace.

Moments later there was the sound of a scuffle. Aurelius signalled a halt, and went back to find out what had happened. About a hundred paces behind the last mule he found Publius with his sword at the throat of a plump, red-faced individual who was expostulating loudly at his rough treatment. "How dare you insult a man of the cloth!" he spluttered.

"Pull back your hood," ordered Aurelius. The man did as he was told, and Aurelius saw what he had been looking for – the tonsure. Not the circular bald patch of the Roman church but the shaved band of the Celtic church. So far so good.

"Dominus Vobiscum," said Aurelius.

"Et cum spiritu tuo," replied the man without hesitation.

"Put up your sword, Publius," said Aurelius. "The man is genuine. Otherwise he would not have known the correct response."

Then, turning to the monk, he said, "Why are you following us?"

"I am not following you, my lord."

"Then why did you not catch up with us when we slowed down?"

The monk was indignant. "Need you ask! The abbot sends me to Roche Abbey on my own without even a mule to ride on, and when I tell him these are dangerous times, he replies that my cloth will protect me..."

Aurelius looked hard at the man as if looking for a direct answer to his question. The man got the message. "I couldn't decide what to do. I thought of catching you up for the safety of your company – but there is something strange about you – so I decided to keep my distance."

"We are from Gaul," said Aurelius, repeating the magic

word that had worked so well before.

"Ah! Gaul!" said the monk, as though that explained everything.

"Perhaps you will join us now that you know we have nothing to fear," said Aurelius. "Come, walk with me. I want to find out more about the Celtic church."

Aurelius reasoned that, if the man was a spy, he was safer in their company where they could keep an eye on him, and the topic of conversation he had chosen would enable him to confirm that he really was a monk.

Brother Michael, for that was his name, seemed to have little interest in theology, but he knew enough to confirm Aurelius' first impression that he was a genuine monk. He knew all about the Pelagian heresy that had so recently split the church in Britannia, but was more concerned about the cellarer in Roche Abbey, whom he was convinced was cheating the monks out of their rations.

At length, the travellers began the ascent into the Peak District, an area of low mountains, worn by millennia of erosion. The woodland gave way to low scrub and jagged outcrops of rock; the road became steeper and ever-more winding. Sometimes a gap in the rocks allowed a momentary glimpse of the country below, where a winding river made its way through a wooded valley. The pace of the mules became slower and slower, but it was still too much for Brother Michael who began to huff and puff and slowly fall behind. Aurelius warned him that they couldn't wait for him because they needed to get to Edale before nightfall. Slowly, Brother Michael fell behind, and Aurelius gave no more thought to him.

Edale was the last village before the mountainous wastelands, but it was a small settlement and there were no inns. However, the travellers managed to persuade a farmer to let them use his barn for the night. At least it was private, and that is just what Aurelius needed for the announcement he planned to make.

When they had rested and finished their simple meal, Aurelius decided it was time to speak: "Masgwid tells me that tomorrow we will begin to ascend the Pennines, and you will need to know what we are looking for. The clue says that the sword is 'in a rocky place' – that's why we have come to the Pennines, and that is 'guarded by two ogres'. Now, I don't believe in fairy tales, so I think that what we are looking for are rock formations in the shape of ogres."

His companions were tired, and seemed more interested in taking their rest than discussing cryptic clues from dusty old books – all except Gruffen. He was suddenly alert, and began to ask searching questions: "Do you mean carved ogres?" he asked, "like gargoyles on a church?"

"I doubt it," said Aurelius, "That would be too obvious. I imagine a sort of narrow pass with weather-beaten rocks on either side that look a bit like ogres – then we will probably have to dig. That's why we brought shovels."

There was one other clue mentioned in the text, but for some reason Aurelius decided to hold it back. It seemed to be the most insignificant of all the clues – 'across a river' – but it might help to identify the correct rock formation. Nevertheless, he felt compelled to hide something. He knew that he ought to be feeling eagerness and excitement now that the quest was about to begin for real, but if anything, he felt downcast. The clue, that he had just told the others, seemed vaguer than ever. Hundreds of miles of rocks, and they had to look for a formation that looked like ogres – almost any jagged lump of rock could be shaped by the imagination into anything. And if they found the rocks – what then? Where should they dig, and how deep? Then he remembered Brother Michael. There was no doubt in his mind that he was a real monk. But why was he travelling alone? Why did he try to avoid them, and why did he – so slyly it seemed now – slip away. Was he a spy, after all? A real monk, yes, but sent by Marcus to find out where they were going. Perhaps he had stayed on their trail even after he had fallen behind, and was even now hanging around in the darkness, waiting to follow them on the morrow. The others discussed the clues for while and then settled themselves down in the straw to sleep. Aurelius did likewise.

He lay awake for a long time listening to the contented breathing of his companions while a thousand troubles flitted about in his restless mind. At last he slipped into a troubled sleep in which he dreamed that Vortigern's spies followed him over a barren landscape on a futile quest which ended with an empty hole in the ground.

Publius' voice awoke him. "Gruffen is gone," he said.

Aurelius sat up quickly. "Gruffen?" and as he repeated the name, a dozen of Gruffen's suspicious actions flashed through his mind: the way he had begged to be part of the quest, even though he had not offered his support at the council. The way he had continually questioned him about their route, the way he had asked to know the clue, long before it was needed. "What a fool I was!" he gasped, "and I thought he was harmless..."

"He knows the clue," said Masgwid , "and he has run off to tell Vortigern."

Aurelius gave a hollow laugh. "Well I hope he can make more sense of it than I can! Uther was right. It is like looking for a needle in a haystack – and we don't really know what we are looking for, the clue is so vague!"

Aurelius felt some slight consolation when he remembered that he had held back a small part of it – perhaps that part might turn out to be significant.

"Vague clues have habit of seeming very precise when you have solved them," said Masgwid , "and we have to try."

"Well, we'd better get started," said Publius. "These hills will be crawling with Vortigern's men in a day or two."

"I'll lead the way," said Masgwid. "From here on we will be following the old footways. Luckily, we will cross the border into Elmet soon, and I know those footways like the back of my hand."

The way was steep, stark and stony, with howling winds which hammered on their bodies, wailing like a banshee of the woes of Albion. Soon they were above the treeline, and the footway wound agonisingly between rocky outcrops. Masgwid and Pubius, scrutisised each one, trying to make out a resemblance to ogres until their eyes ached. Before long, Aurelius decided it was time to put them out of their misery. During the next rest break he told them the text in full:

> *The sword is in a rocky place in Logres,*
> *across a river, guarded by two ogres.*

"Gruffen doesn't know about the river," he added. "I don't suppose it makes much difference, but you can save your eyes, until we come to a river."

"I know these hills inside out," said Masgwid . "There's no river up here!"

"No, of course, not," said Aurelius, "but the source of a river – a stream."

"Hundreds of them!" said Masgwid with a sigh.

II

That night they could find nowhere to shelter except a tumble-down shepherd's bothy where they made themselves as comfortable as they could. At least they were out of the howling wind. Throughout the night, the storm got worse, and their humble shelter trembled in the force of the gale. Rain leaked through the rotten thatch and soaked them to the skin. Nevertheless, Aurelius slept well. There was something comforting in the storm. While it raged away outside, he had no fear of his enemies taking him by surprise.

They awoke to a fresh, bright morning which raised everybody's spirits. "Surely there must be someone around here we can ask. The local folk will know if there are any strange rock formations."

"This is sheep country," said Masgwid . "The soil is too acid for crops, but the grass provides grazing. The shepherds follow their sheep from place to place and sleep in simple bothies like our palace of last night."

Sure enough, it was not long before they saw a shepherd in the distance. Masgwid hailed him, and he approached warily. A few words from Masgwid in the local Elmet dialect were enough to reassure the man, and soon he was talking freely, seeming to enjoy the chance of conversation and company. After a few pleasantries, Masgwid came to the point: "Have you seen a rock, or other thing in the shape of an ogre?"

The shepherd answered with a wry smile, "Ogre? Only my wife's mother!"

"Perhaps then, you know of a stream nearby?"

The shepherd waved his hand in a northerly direction. "Just keep going and you'll come to a stream. They say its the source of the river Don, but whatever it is, I wish the wife's mother would jump in it and leave me in peace!"

They went in the direction the shepherd had indicated and noticed that the ground began to slope into a kind of depression. Soon the turf began to squelch under their feat, and in the distance they could see the silver gleam of a winding stream. Not far away, a crofter was digging peat to fuel his fire, so Masgwid asked him the same questions.

"Ogre? well, my old grandsire told a story of two troll-kind; Grendel and his ogre mother – that's all I've heard of trolls and ogres. I don't know of any other."

"Where is Grendel?" asked Masgwid .

"At Coningsburg, in the cliffs – a rocky place – well, that's what you said you were looking for."

"You say a rocky place?"

"Yes that's where the troll lives."

"Where's Coningsburg?"

"You're from around here, aren't you? It's the place we used to called Caer Conan, but Hengest and the Angles hold it now. If you are wise you will keep away!"

"You are right! May Camulus strike him dead!" In his anger, Masgwid had invoked one of the pre-Christian gods. He quickly corrected himself, "I mean, the Lord of Hosts, of course."

Aurelius said, "Caer Conan. Is that not the citadel that was built by my ancestor Conan Meriadoc, the man who later founded Armorica?"

"One and the same."

"And it is in Saxon hands?"

"They are Angles, but they are all of the same hell-spawned race. Hengest is their leader, and Caer Conan — Coningsburg, as he now calls it — is his base."

The crofter listened in confusion to these grand historical references and wondered what kind of people he was dealing with. His question was soon answered.

"Do you know who I am?" said Masgwid.

"No, my lord," said the Crofter, fearing trouble.

"I am Masgwid, King of Elmet. This is my seal." He showed him the large ring on his left hand. The crofter had no idea what Masgwid or his seal should look like, but the man's overbearing demeanour was sufficient. He knelt, kissed the seal and said, "My lord, I am at your service."

"If anyone else asks you the same questions, send them in the opposite direction. Publius, give the man a token of our goof will."

Publius took a handful of assari from his purse and gave them to the crofter.

The man stuttered his thanks, and took his leave, forgetting to take his peat in his eagerness to get away from these mighty people, whose recent generosity might turn to anger just as quickly as sunshine turned to storm.

"What do you think of his story?" said Masgwid.

"An old wives' tale, a myth, but..."

"My lord..." said Publius, a note of alarm in his voice. "Look!"

Far down the valley to the west could be seen a crowd of about twenty small figures. The occasional glint suggested sunlight reflected on metal – in other words, armour!

"Vortigern's men, most likely. We cannot stay here!" said Masgwid. "But which way shall we go?"

"We will follow the stream," said Aurelius.

"To investigate an old wives' tale," said Masgwid. "That was what you called it."

"I was about to say that old wives' tales – legends – are usually based on something. I don't know what, but there is just a chance that the legend of the trolls is based on the legend of the Sword."

"What do you mean?"

"I don't know. But as there are no large rock formations around this particular stream, I think Caer Conan is our best lead at the moment."

"But it is in the heart of Angle territory!" protested Masgwid.

"Well, it's the Angles or Vortigern," said Aurelius with a glance down into the valley.

"I'll take the Angles," said Masgwid. "They're further away!"

They made their way into the lowlands, working slowly east, following the river Don as best as they could until they were close to Caer Conan. By this time, the Don had spread into a broad river. They followed it for several miles, but there was no sign of any rocks, only a gently undulating countryside, richly wooded, and broken up here and there by the characteristic strip farms of the Angles. They passed many peasants and farm workers, but humble merchants, wearing what were by now rather ragged and soiled robes, and leading tired-looking mules, were hardly worthy of their attention.

"Where's that cliff the crofter spoke of?" said Masgwid, looking round the valley.

"I wish we had Gruffen here. We could do with his Anglisc," said Aurelius feeling, as he said the words, less angry with himself for having brought him along.

"No need, look!" said Publius.

There was a patch of white in the undergrowth about 500 paces from the other side of the river, and as they walked on, the land rose, and the patch of white grew into a magnificent limestone cliff.

"But how do we cross?" said Masgwid.

"There must be a boat we can 'borrow' or a ferry."

They came to a place where the river made a wide turn to the north. To their right was a high eminence with a hill fort on its summit.

"Caer Conan," said Masgwid. "It was a border hill fort between the Brigantes and Coritanes in the days before the Romans came. It looks as though Hengest has refortified it."

"Can they see us?" said Aurelius.

"Probably. But what do they see? Three merchants and four mules. Hardly a reason to turn out the guard. You were right not to bring a large force."

Using the ferry was going to be awkward. Masgwid thought they could carry it off with grunts and sign language. Aurelius thought it might be better to pass by and try to find a boat. The matter was decided by the ferryman, who waved them on board. He wished them good day in the Angle tongue, and helped them to lead their mules onto the raft. Then, with a long pole, he pushed out into the river. As he poled, he sang a song. The song was a Brythonic lament.

"You are a Briton?" said Masgwid.

The man nodded and carried on with his song.

"So much the better, perhaps you can help us. Have you heard the legend of Grendel the troll?"

The man stopped singing and seemed to collect his thoughts. "There is a song about Grendel. Do you want to hear it?"

"Just tell me what you know."

"The song tells of two trolls, Grendel and his dam, who live in the caves yonder. It is said that they guard a sword of fabulous worth."

Aurelius was suddenly alert, "A sword!"

The ferryman laughed. "Aye, and many a Tom-fool has scratched around in those caves looking for it. Well, I'll tell you the truth. I looked for it myself when I was a lad, and I can tell you for a fact that the caves go on for about a hundred paces, and then come to a dead end – nothing."

Aurelius was mumbling like one in a delirium: "Across a river, guarded by two ogres, two caves – this is it!"

The ferryman continued laughing. "Aye, that's it, it is has driven many a man mad. Well, here you are. That will be an assarius for each of you, and for the mules."

He took the coins which Publius gave him, and still chuckling to himself, started to pole back across the river. When he had got halfway, he suddenly started to pole faster, and shouted at the top of his voice in the Angle language. It didn't need an interpreter to understand what he was shouting: "Britons! Help! Britons! Call out the guard!"

"Quickly!" cried Publius. "We have a chance if we hurry. It will take a while for the guards to get to the river, and the ferry is slow. Run!"

"Which way?" said Aurelius.

"There is an abbey not too far off where we can get sanctuary," Masgwid said.

"They're heathens, so it won't make any difference," said Aurelius. "We'll have to lose them!"

"It's goodbye to the mules then," said Masgwid sadly.

"Come on!" urged Publius, and soon they were jogging along the riverbank. They rounded the bend in the river, and to their relief, the hill fort was hidden from their sight, which, of course, meant that the lookouts couldn't see them.

"We need to cross again!" gasped Masgwid who was struggling to keep up. There were no more ferries, so they had no option but to swim. They made bundles of their clothes as quickly as they could and jumped into the freezing water. Masgwid, who was a poor swimmer, managed to get across with the help of a log. For several miles, they kept to the undergrowth, but when their clothing had dried off a little, Aurelius said, "I think we can risk travelling by road now. We lost our pursuers when we re-crossed the river. I am sure they will have gone straight on to Danecaster."

"How can a Christian monastery survive in an Angle kingdom?" said Aurelius.

Masgwid explained. "Roche Abbey is across the border in Pengwern. The border is marked by a large swathe of swampy ground. There is a footway that crosses it, but those who don't know the footway will be up to their necks in slime before they have gone ten paces. In any case, there is peace treaty that marks their boundary with Elmet as the Icknield Way, and the boundary with Pengwern as the swamp."

The land sloped uphill for a few miles through thickly wooded country. They saw few people, a forester chopping wood, a woman gathering berries, a small boy leading a cow, all of whom took no notice of three men who looked as poor as themselves. They skirted a village, and then the land began to fall away. Soon the ground was soft beneath their feet. "From here on, you must follow my footsteps exactly," warned Masgwid.

They picked their way carefully through the marsh and

waded across a shallow river, which Masgwid said was called Maltby Beck. Aurelius heard the sound of chanting voices, and looking up, saw a small cluster of buildings which he took to be Roche Abbey. In the centre of the cluster was a building with a large wooden cross on the gable. This was the abbey church. As they got closer, Aurelius recognised the service as Compline, the final service of the day, and decided that it would do no harm if they let themselves into the church and joined in the service. When the service was over, they would request hospitality for the night. Aurelius had no definite plan beyond that, but he knew that he must wait a few days for the dust to settle, then they would find a way to go back to the cliffs at Caer Conan and look for Excalibur.

The monks were chanting in the chancel, and in the nave the Christian brothers knelt in prayer, solemn and hooded, among them, a few villagers. Aurelius knelt and prayed with fervour, although not for himself alone. Hearing the phrase: "Pacem in terris", he prayed for peace in Albion. Incense drifted from the censer, candle smoke rose in the air. Monks sang "Gloria in excelsis", and the Lord answered his prayer: he looked up to the chancel archway and hanging from the arch's keystone, he saw a wooden cross suspended. On the capitals of the pillars on either side were two carvings; gargoyle heads – demons, monsters, or by another name – ogres!

Aurelius heart began to race, his hands trembled, his breath came in quick gasps. I am going mad, he thought. I am overtired. I must consider it calmly. He made an effort to control himself. He clenched his fists and slowed his breathing. Then he recited the text to himself:

The sword is in a rocky place in Logres,
across a river, guarded by two ogres.

'A rocky place'? – 'Roche' was the Brythonic word for

rock, so 'Roche Abbey' meant the 'abbey of the rock'. Perhaps the rocky place had nothing to do with cliffs and mountains after all. The next line, which was the heart of the puzzle, because it had seemed so unimportant was now easy to unlock: it was not 'across' but 'a cross'. There was the cross right before his eyes. The river? Well that was Maltby Beck that they crossed after the marsh. As for the ogres, well, the gargoyle faces were plain enough! Aurelius felt a renewed burst of excitement. He told himself he must wait until the service was over, but he seemed to have no control over the trembling hand that reached for "Hope". He swung the blade at the hanging wooden cross, which splintered into many pieces and fell onto the reredos. Lay brother guardians sprung to action at the abbot's urgent word, and knocked his sword out of his hand, but there beside it on the pavement lay another sword: four foot long, a hilt of silver with five rubies, the blade glittering with words of gold – Excalibur which legends sang through the long centuries.

Aurelius lifted his gaze to another, larger, cross at the end of the chancel, and cried out in a loud voice: "I have the sword! I am king!"

But no cheer arose from the monks, only a warning shout. Aurelius heard it too late. He felt a sharp blow to his head and fell to the ground, stunned. As he fell, the sword was snatched up by a stranger's hand.

Aurelius came to his senses in time to see Gruffen waving the sword in the air shouting, "No! I have the sword! I am king!"

A crowd of Vortigern's men had by this time filled the church. Their leader spoke up: "The sword is for Vortigern! Give it up! No-one will accept a worthless wretch like you as king!"

With these words, he tried to grab him, but Gruffen fended him off with the sword, and escaped through the chancel door before the others could catch him.

"Quickly!" shouted the leader, whom the monks recognised as Morcant. "First decani, this way. The others, go round."

Behind the Abbey was a lake, and it was towards this that Gruffen ran. When he reached it, he hesitated whether to turn right or left. He looked round to gauge where the his best chance lay, and saw men approaching from both sides, not far behind them came the Abbot, the monks, Masgwid, Publius, and Aurelius, his splitting headache not diminishing his desire to witness Gruffen's fate.

Seeing that escape was impossible, Gruffen turned around and pleaded with his pursuers: "I will make a better king than Vortigern. I..."

His words turned into a scream as Morcant's sword plunged into his stomach. He staggered with the impact of the blow, but then with his a last gasp of strength, he turned and flung the sword into the lake. The blade whirled through the air, flashing reflections of the last rays of the dying sun, and plunging into the dark water with a great splash that glittered with the ruddy rays, like a shower of blood. Some of the monks swore afterwards that they saw an arm clothed with white samite catch the sword and pull it below the surface – but perhaps it was just the sun's rays catching on the blade.

Aurelius became aware of Masgwid pulling at his sleeve. "Come on! Let's try to get away while they are distracted."

And distracted they were. Some of them were standing around Gruffen's body, all talking at once, while others tried to wade into the lake, each hoping to find the sword – most of them for the honour of presenting it to Vortigern, a few, like Gruffen, wanted it for themselves. They didn't get far, for the bottom sloped away sharply. Indeed, the monks, along with several other pagan beliefs, such as a belief in the Lady of the Lake, were convinced that the lake was bottomless. They held back at a respectful distance from Vortigern's men, and the three travellers were hidden amongst them. They were just about to break away from the group and return to the church, when the abbot stopped them.

"My lords," he said, "come with me. The best place to hide is in a crowd. I will dress you in monks' robes and you will be better hidden than among the trees of Sherwood."

Aurelius took one final look over his shoulder before the abbot hurried them inside the dormitory. A boat had been found, and Vortigern's men were making attempts to dive for the sword. At the same time, their leader was giving orders for the lake to be cordoned off and guarded.

While Aurelius and his fellow travellers shuffled into monk's habits, and a brother shaved their heads. The abbot had arranged a further distraction. A young monk, at his instructions, went up to Morcant and said, "I am an accomplished swimmer. If anyone can dive to the bottom of the lake. I can."

Morcant gave his agreement, and the monk shrugged off his robe, revealing a body as well-muscled as a young athlete, which brought gasps of admiration from some of the onlookers. He was rowed to the place where the sword was last seen, and after taking several deep breaths he disappeared beneath the surface. Just when it seemed he was gone forever, his head appeared several yards away from the boat. He gasped for breath, and shouted, "I have the sword!"

A great cheer went up from the watchers. Even the monks cheered, though some of the older and wiser amongst them guessed what was happening. A moment later, the young monk held an object high in the air. It was, indeed, a sword, but a sorrier and more rusted item you have never seen.

The watchers jeered. Morcant's began to suspect he was being made to look a fool. Then the full realisation of what had happened in the church hit him. "Where is the man?" he said, turning and scanning the crowd of onlookers. They knew whom he meant – the man who had found Excalibur – they didn't know it was Aurelius, but they believed him to be his agent.

"Search the abbey!" ordered Morcant. "Don't allow anyone to leave!"

They searched the abbey, but found only monks and lay brothers. "They must have got away," said one of his men. "Shall we go after them?"

"Yes. Follow the road to Sherwood. That's where I would go if I were them. And send to Vortigern for more men. We will drain that lake if we have to – but whatever it takes, we will find the sword."

III

Aurelius slept badly that night, mainly because of the wound on his head. Which seemed worse than it did at the time when the blow fell, and throbbed as though his skull would burst. He was awoken by the bell for the midnight office, and despite the throbbing in his head, thought he had better attend. He noticed that Masgwid and Publius slept through it, though no-one seemed to notice. Morcant had posted men at the back of the church, but they were half asleep, and didn't bother to count the monks, so the service proceeded without event, and Aurelius was soon able to lower himself gratefully onto his pallet bed. The next bell was for Matins. This time the church was full. Vortigern's men were standing in the side aisles, and Morcant himself was counting. He soon discovered that there were more of them than there should be.

"There are three more monks than are recorded on your roll," he said. "I want those three to step forward now, or every brother in this church will be put to the question!"

There was a shocked silence. They all knew that "put to the question" was a euphemism for "torture".

Aurelius stepped forward. Masgwid and Publius hesitated, but a moment later, did the same. Morcant looked hard at Aurelius. His steely grey eyes promising harm.

"So, you are the man who found the sword – the agent of the pretender, Aurelius!"

"I am," said Aurelius coolly.

"Well, men," said Morcant, a malicious smile on his face. "What shall we do with him?"

Aurelius took another step forward so that he was in full view of everyone in the church. "The question is – what shall I do with you, who dare to challenge your rightful king? I am Aurelius Ambrosius, the eldest son of Constantine the Fair, and by right of descent, the High King of Britannia."

Gasps of surprise came from monks and soldiers alike.

"Vortigern is our king!" said Morcant.

"Vortigern is a usurper!" said Aurelius.

"And perhaps you are another! What proof can you offer?"

It was the question that had haunted Aurelius for decades, but now he had the answer. He opened his cloak and held up the Sword.

Shouts of amazement came from all sides: "Excalibur! But how is it possible? I saw it thrown into the lake with my own eyes! Is it magic? Is it the work of the Lady of the Lake?"

The abbot was quick to overrule these old Celtic superstitions: "It is the hand of God!" he roared, and with those words, he knelt before Aurelius and bowed his head. Now all attention was fixed on Morcant. He hesitated for a moment, perhaps calculating his chances – how many of his men might go over to Aurelius? Who would best repay his loyalty? It was not a difficult decision. He knelt, holding up his sword to Aurelius, and his men followed suit.

A great cheer went up from the monks, and Vortigern's,

now Aurelius' men, got to their feet and joined in. The rejoicing went on for some time, until a different voice was heard, calling for attention.

"Brothers! Brothers!" it was the abbot. The clamour gradually subsided and the abbot continued: "Brothers, let us not forget why we are here. The purpose of our lives is to offer up prayer, and Matins has not yet been said. Let us kneel and begin our service now, and I will say a special prayer for Aurelius, High King of Britannia, who found Excalibur in our own humble church, and will use it to bring peace on earth and good well to all men."

EPILOGUE

In later times, Aurelius was often asked how he came to be possessed of a sword which so many had seen with their own eyes had been cast into the lake. This was his reply: "That night I had a dream, and in that dream a beautiful lady appeared to me who said, 'I am the Lady of the Lake, and I am bringing the sword to its rightful owner. Guard it well.' In my dream, she gave me Excalibur and when I awoke, my own sword was gone and Excalibur was in its place."

Of course, there were many who, sceptical of mystery and magic, said that Gruffen, in his frenzy, simply grabbed the wrong sword and threw that into the lake. Whatever the truth behind the story, Aurelius, would only smile and repeat his version. He knew that a little myth and magic, a bottomless pool and the Lady of the Lake would do much to enhance the aura that now surrounded him. Above all, he had Excalibur, and his kingship of Britannia was beyond question. Now the Britons could unite and drive their enemies from the realm of Albion.

3. A CONINGSBURGH LAD AT THE BATTLE OF LINCOLN

William de Warenne, 3ʳᵈ Earl of Surrey (1119-1148) was Lord of Conisbrough Castle during that terrible time known as The Anarchy, when England was torn apart by the competing forces of King Stephen and the Empress Matilda. One of the key battles of The Anarchy was the Battle of Lincoln, in which De Warenne and his men played an important part. This story describes that battle from the point of view of a young blacksmith who aspires to be a man-at-arms. It is part of a novel-in-progress provisionally entitled Crusader, as De Warenne and his squire later take part in the Second Crusade.

I

Robert was pumping away at the bellows for all he was worth while his master held a circle of wrought iron in pair of tongs over the blazing forge. Both of them were pouring with sweat, and the heat was beginning to sear Robert's face, but he daren't stop now, or the process would have to begin again. The blacksmith, whose name was Brom, watched the colour of the metal intently, waiting for that cherry red glow that signalled it was ready to forge. He was a bear of a man, with biceps bigger than Robert's head, and fists like sledgehammers. His neck was thick and short, so that his grizzled beard, though short, hung on chest. His features were strong and his expression stern, as you might expect from a man who had spent a lifetime wrestling with that most stubborn of materials. His skin was weathered by exposure to heat and smoke, and at that moment, though Robert was ready to faint, he didn't seem to feel the heat at all.

Robert, though only 14, was as big as Brom and almost as muscular. He had started work at the smithy when he was 8, and years of heavy work had built up his physique until it was like a prize-fighter's. However, his smooth, young face, and bright blues showed that he was a dreamer at heart.

At last, judging the colour to be right, Brom whisked the circle of red-hot iron from the forge to a metal former and started to beat it with a fuller with quick, deft strokes, the first part in the long process of shaping the circle of wrought iron into a conical helmet.

Meanwhile, Robert had stopped working the bellows and gone to the door, which was always left wide open, to get a breath of fresh air.

"Keep at them bellows, now, lad," said Brom, "I shall be wantin' t' forge again in minute."

Robert sighed, went back to the bellows and started to work them. A moment later, Brom brought the work back to the forge, and the process began again. But this time, Brom had no sooner begun the hammering, when a little black dog shot out from the back kitchen, ran between Brom's legs, and straight out of the front door into West Street.

The half-formed helmet dropped onto the floor with a clatter, no longer cherry red, but still dangerously hot, and missing Brom's foot by mere inches.

"By God's Bones!" roared Brom. "What was that?"

"It's only Toby," said Robert apologetically.

"What's that runt doin' in 'ere, anyway?" said Brom. "If ah see 'im again ah'll roast 'im!"

"Sorry, master. 'Ee must 'ave escaped from t' back kitchen," said Robert, putting down the bellows, and hurrying to the door to look for Toby.

"Where does tha think tha's guin'?" snapped Brom. "There's wok to do 'ere! Me lord wants these 'elmets next week, not next year!"

"Sorry, master."

But the fire in the forge was burning low, and the half-formed helmet was cold. Brom sighed, shook his head and decided to make the best of it.

"Well we've been at it all mornin'. We'll tek a break nah."

He turned and called to the other side of the forge, where two junior apprentices were laboriously unpicking a battered mail hauberk.

"Come on, Tom. Come Dick. We're tekin' a break."

They went into the back kitchen where the blacksmith's daughter, Mildred, a girl of about 11, was stirring a pot which hung over the kitchen fire.

"Yer early!" she said, looking up.

"Aye, an that's dog's to blame!"

"Toby! Where is 'ee?"

Her question was answered by a little "wuff" from the kitchen door.

"Cat got away, I suppose," said Brom.

Mildred left the pot to give Toby the welcome he didn't deserve. He was a disreputable looking mongrel, with black fur, a white patch over one eye, short, stubby legs, one ear that stuck up, and another ear, mangled in a fight, hanging down – but Mildred loved him, though the unappreciative Toby had settled his affection on Robert, whom he regarded as his master.

"Where's yer mother?" said Brom.

"In't leather shop. Ah'll fetch 'er."

Brom's smithy was the largest in Coningsburgh. It was a long, single-storey building constructed of roughly-coursed magnesian limestone with a tall chimney for the forge. He employed three apprentices, of whom Robert was the senior.

Round the back was an extension built of wood, which were the living quarters. To one side was another extension, also of wood, where Brom had a small leather shop. Here all the leather goods linked to his trade were made; saddles, helmet linings, gambesons, and assorted straps, belts and harnesses. His wife, Alice, oversaw the shop, though the work was done by two apprentices.

There was one other blacksmith in Coningsburgh who had a small forge in the Inner Bailey of the castle, but he confined himself to small jobs and repairs, as he had neither the space nor the manpower to do the big jobs such as manufacturing armour.

Robert spooned down his soup with relish, not forgetting to dip a hunk of bread in the soup and throw it to Toby. A mug of small beer completed the repast, and after a few moments lounging at the kitchen table, Brom got up to go back to work.

"Tom, ah want thee on t' forge. Robert, tha can gu dahn to't castle an' fetch them 'auberks that want mendin'. Oh, an tek the 'andcart. Dobbin is up in Top Field today."

Brom left the kitchen, then, remembering something, thrust his head round the door jamb and said, "Mildred, keep that blasted dog out o' t' forge!"

Robert took the handcart and started off along High Street, which was almost opposite the forge. A "wuff" told him that he had got company. Toby had decided to follow him. Well, at least he was out of his master's way. Robert went past the church to where High Street joins Church Street, from which point he had a good view of the castle.

The castle at the time of our story was not very different from what we see today. The walls and the towers were the same, though there was no barbican. The main difference was the keep. The magnificent six-buttressed, ashlar-faced edifice that is the castle's crowning glory had yet to be built, and in its place was a smaller round donjon built in the same roughly-coursed limestone as the walls.

Even from this distance Robert could see that it was as busy as usual – which was only to be expected, as it was only a year ago that the Empress Matilda and Robert of Gloucester had rebelled against King Stephen and had gained control of the south-west of England. Most of the northern lords, including Sir William de Warenne, 3rd Earl of Surrey and lord of Coningsburgh Castle, supported the king, and were preparing for the inevitable confrontation.

It was not long before Robert came to the gatehouse of the castle's Outer Bailey. This was a wooden construction intended as a first line of defence, but nowhere near as strong as the mighty stone walls that loomed behind it.

The foot serjeant on duty recognized Robert immediately. " 'Ey up, Robert. Tha allreet?"

Robert nodded, and took a moment to appraise the foot serjeant's arms and armour. He was wearing a nasal helmet over a mail coif, and a short, sleeveless mail hauberk under his jupon, which was resplendent with the De Warenne chequers of gold and blue, or to express it in heraldic language, *chequy or and azure*. Around his waist was a leather belt from which hung a broad, heavy sword at his left hand side, and a short dagger at the right. His legs, unlike those of the mounted men-at-arms, were unarmoured, being protected only by hose of thick leather. In his right hand he held a voulge, a polearm with a slender axe-head ending in spike.

Robert's interest was the result of his secret ambition –

to become a foot-serjeant, or even a man-at-arms one day. It was not an easy ambition to achieve, because foot serjeants were expected to provide their own arms and armour before being hired by a lord.

They exchanged a few commonplaces then the foot serjeant called to the gatekeeper. "Open up. It's Robert."

Robert could remember a time when the Outer Gatehouse was always open, and had only the gatekeeper to guard it – but in those troubled times every precaution had to be taken. Robert went through the gate with Toby at his heels. Nobody challenged Toby, though as we have seen, he was quite capable of causing trouble.

There were two guards on the main gate, and though they also knew Robert, they were too near to their master's scrutiny to dispense with formalities. Their halberds crossed and barred his way, and one of them gave the challenge: "Halt! Who goes there?"

"It's me, Robert."

He didn't mention Toby, and once again he slipped in unnoticed. It's fortunate that he wasn't a spy – but Toby was as loyal to his king as any dog in England.

Robert went straight to the smithy, which was situated in the range of buildings against the north wall. It was a smaller version of the smithy on West Street, worked by a smith called Adam and one apprentice.

" 'Ello Robert," said Adam. "Tha's come fer them 'auberks ah reckon."

"Ah," replied Robert (which then as now is a Conisbrough way of saying "yes").

"Well, 'ere they is, and they's in a reet state ah can tell yer! They was ripped to bits in some battle an' then chucked in t' dungeon, an' nah they's rusty as well. But me lord needs all t' armour he can get, so do wot yer can. Oh an' theer's a rusty ol' 'elmet, an' all."

Robert examined the hauberks, but their dilapidated state did not worry him. Indeed he saw an opportunity to further a little project of his own, which was to make a hauberk of his own. A hauberk was one of the most expensive items in a foot serjeant's outfit. Not only was the iron expensive, the labour involved in riveting together all those tiny rings was much more so – however, Robert could do the work himself; it was getting hold of the iron that was difficult, but he reckoned that, with these hauberks in such a state, there was bound to be a good number of links left over.

A commotion outside the smithy interrupted Robert's reflections. It was as though a hundred dogs were barking at once, and among them, Robert recognized the bark of Toby. He ran out of the smithy to find a writhing heap of dogs with two people trying to break them up. One was Simon the Fewterer, who was trying to discipline the two bloodhounds for which he was responsible. The other was a little girl of about seven dressed in court clothes. Robert recognized her as Isabel, Sir William's daughter. She was pretty, in a childish way, but her long dress with its stiff embroidering and lace trimmings made her look rather like a doll. Nevertheless, she was the nearest thing to a princess that could be see in Coningsburgh because Isabel de Warenne was Sir William's only child and the heiress to vast estates in Coningsburgh, Castle Acre, Lewes and Reigate.

It seemed that her lapdog, a small brown and white spaniel, had managed to escape from the keep, only to be set upon by the bloodhounds that the fewterer was bringing to Sir William. Toby, who loved a fight, had felt it his duty to intervene.

By the time Robert got there, the fight had already been brought under control. The bloodhounds had been called to heel, and Isabel had picked up her spaniel, who was called Bijou, and was trying to comfort her. Robert summoned Toby, but Toby chose to ignore him – not being a very well-disciplined dog. Robert, therefore, picked him up roughly by the scruff of the neck.

"Ne pas lui faire du mal," said Isabel. "Il a sauvé Bijou."

It took Robert a moment to adjust his mind to her court French, and even then, he understood it but poorly. However, he realized that she was asking him not to hurt Toby because he had saved Bijou. Robert was keen to learn French, as he knew it was a necessary accomplishment for a foot serjeant, and he had tried to pick up as much as he could. He racked his brains for a reply, but nothing came, so he merely nodded. Then, with stern word to Toby, he put him down and gave him a firm push in the direction of the gatehouse. He would have gone back to the smithy just then, but Isabel wanted to say more. She rattled on and on in French, and Robert understood enough to realise that she – and Bijou – were eternally grateful, and that he might call on her if he ever needed help with anything. She was only a child, thought Robert, but child or not, it is useful to have friends in high places. So he smiled, bowed, chucked Bijou under the chin, and managed to splutter, "C'est un gentil chien." Saying that Bijou was a 'nice dog' was probably the best thing he could have said even if he had been attending French lessons for years. Isabel gave him a broad smile and a moment later was hurrying up the steep steps to the keep with Bijou waddling behind her.

II

When Robert got back to the forge, he showed the hauberks and helmet to Brom, who shook his head and said, "Well, we might mek one good un' out o' these two. As for this 'elmet, there's not much left o' it."

"Can I 'ave t' leftover mail?" asked Robert.

"Aye, though it wain't be much good."

"It'll do."

"Still want ter be a man-at-arms?"

Robert looked uncomfortable. He knew that the other apprentices laughed at him behind his back.

48

"There's more to bein' a man-at-arms than a home-made 'auberk, tha knows," said Brom. "Yer've got ter provide all yer own equipment, includin' a 'oss – and yer knows how much one o' them costs!"

"Well, maybe ah'll be a foot serjeant, then," mumbled Robert.

"Tha's still got to 'ave a lot o' expensive kit – an' yer need trainin' as well. Nah, if yer'll tek my advice, yer'll stick to yer trade – an' a good un' it is, too."

Brom looked hard at Robert, who looked away. It was clear that nothing could make him change his mind.

"Well, let's see what we can do abaht this 'elmet. You can fix it, an' I'll help yer."

"I thought yer said there were not much left o' it," said Robert. "So 'ow can we fix it?"

"We can mek it into a spangenhelm," said Brom. "Yer see, it's a rounded 'elmet, so we can put iron bands front ter back an' side ter side, an' fill in t' gaps wi' new pieces. It's much easier ter shape a piece o' a 'elmet than t' whole thing, so it's a good bit o' practice fer thee. When thas med the bands an' t' pieces, we just rivet it all together. It wain't be as good as a one-piece job, but it'll be good enough."

"Can ah keep it?"

Brom frowned.

"Nay, lad. There's too much metal in there to give to thee, and Constable Heydon'll be expecting it back."

Brom showed him how to heat the metal to the right shade of cherry red and then hammer it by holding it against the former and striking just off centre.

"If tha hit's t' metal against t' former it'll thin it. We dunna want ter thin it, we wants ter bend it, so mek sure yer tap it just off centre."

Robert was clumsy at first, but bit by bit, he got the feel of it, and was proud to see the stubborn material bend to his will.

It was slow work, and before Robert knew it, Brom was

calling his apprentices to stop work and go to the back kitchen for a bite to eat.

"An abaht time too," muttered Tom.

"Ah heard yer!" said Brom, "but dunna fret, ah'm thinkin' o' tekin' on another 'prentice."

"We need one," said Robert, "we can 'ardly keep up with t' work!"

"Aye, well we've King Stephen ter thank fo' that," said Brom. "Ah don't know whether ah prefer peaceful times an' a quiet forge, or troubled times like these when ah can 'ardly keep up wi' t' werk!"

Robert had his own opinion. He preferred troubled times – all the more chance of becoming a man-at-arms. But he said nothing.

Since Mrs Smith worked in the leather-shop, she enjoyed the privilege of sitting down at table while Mildred served. Mildred, with the help of a maid-of-all-work, called Bessy, did all the housekeeping and cooking, and this sometimes led the apprentices to forget her privileged position as the daughter of their master.

"Hurry up, Mildred," called Tom, "ah'm gasping for a drink. It's dry work in that forge!"

"Ah'm not your skivvy, Thomas of Melton, and don't you forget it!" snapped Alice as she slammed two pot onto the table, causing the beer to slop over the rims. Tom grinned, and was about to make a jest of it, when he caught his master's disapproving look. A moment later, Mildred had disappeared to fetch two more pots.

"How's t' leather shop?" said Brom to his wife.

"Ah, can 'ardly keep up wi t' work, but ah'm not complaining. We're mekin' a pretty penny!"

"Aye, and there's more men-at-arms at t' castle very day. 'Ope it keeps up!"

After the meal, Robert went out into the backyard and spent an hour at the pell. It was an old wooden gatepost that he had set up as a target for his wooden sword. He tried to copy the cuts that he had learned from the men-at-arms at the castle. Sometimes when he was passing through the Outer Bailey he would watch them practicing, and sometimes one of them would give him a quick lesson – especially if Serjeant Goodlad was elsewhere. One of them had showed him how to use the letter X as a guide. Cut down through the X, both ways, then up through the X, both ways, hitting the pell as hard as possible, and after each stroke, hold the sword in the guard position.

Robert did this as often as he could. In summer, for an hour after work, and in winter, for half an hour during the mid-day break. He imagined he was training himself to be a man-at-arms, not realizing that there was so much more to it than hammering at the pell.

Next day, Robert continued working on the helmet, shaping another two pieces of metal in the same way as before. When the pieces were finished, Brom called Tom to turn the grindstone, and showed Robert how to grind the pieces to a smooth finish. That was followed by the relatively simple process of bending iron bands and drilling holes for the rivets.

That day after work, Robert spent some time on his hauberk – though hauberk was a bit of an exaggeration for the modest mail shirt he was making out of the broken bits of mail he could scrounge. The left-over links from the two hauberks enabled him to extend it down to his waist. It wasn't much, but it was better than nothing, and anyway, it would be covered by the jupon that Mildred was making for him.

"How's it coming on?" he asked her that evening.

"Ah can 'ardly find time ter gu to t' privy, never mind stitch thy jupon!" she teased him, but in fact it was nearly finished. She had been scrounging bits of material for months, dying them blue and yellow, and stitching them together in the chequered pattern that resembled the jupons worn by all of Sir William's men.

"That's gradely!" enthused Robert. "Let me try it on."

"Careful, I've not hemmed it yet."

First, Robert put on his gambeson, which in this case was just a vest made of thick hessian. Then he put on his newly-finished coat of mail. It didn't bear close inspection because the links were of different sizes, and many of them were badly rusted, but that didn't matter because most of the mail shirt would be hidden under the jupon. When he had shuffled into that, he said, "How do I look?"

Mildred was admiring. "Just like a real man-at-arms."

"Wait till that helmet is finished," he said.

"But it's not for you, is it?"

"No, but I'm going to hang on to it as long as I can."

"How?"

"By not finishing it until I need it."

"I don't understand – when will you need it?"

Robert wondered if it was wise to reveal his plan to Mildred. He wasn't afraid of being found out and stopped, but found out and laughed at. Upon consideration he decided that, since Mildred had done so much to help him, she could be trusted with his secret.

"Ah'm guin ter dress up like a proper man-at-arms – well, a foot serjeant, cos I haven't got a oss – and go to Serjeant Dufton at t' castle an' ask if 'ee'll tek me on."

Mildred was wide-eyed at Robert's audacity.

"Do yer think 'ee will?"

"Why not? Ah've hear me lord Warenne is desperate to get as many fightin' men as 'ee can so that 'ee can support King Stephen if it comes to a fight."

"Maybe ah should do t'same," said Mildred.

Robert was aghast. "What! You, a foot serjeant!"

"Neh!" laughed Mildred, playfully slapping his arm. "Ah mean ah should offer mesen to me Lady Adela as a lady-in-waitin'."

She was only joking, but Robert took her seriously.

"It won't work unless yer can speak French."

"Can you?"

"Ah'm learning'. If Serjeant Dufton shouts: "Escouade à droite tournez!" I know that he means: 'Squad right turn!' If he shouts: 'Escouade à gauche tournez!' I know that he means: 'Squad left turn!' and if he shouts: 'Escouade demi-tours tournez!' he means: 'Squad about turn!' An' more than that. I've got to learn to understand everything me lord says, and to answer him properly, too."

"Can yer teach me?"

"Oui,"

"No, ah've just been."

Robert laughed. "No, not 'wee'! 'Oui'! It means 'yes' in French.

Mildred laughed too. Then added in all seriousness. "Ah do want ter learn, yer know, cos ah want ter get on as well. Ah don't want to be a skivvy all me life."

"Ah don't think yer'll ever be a lady-in-waiting," said Robert sympathetically.

Mildred laughed again. "Oh, ah don't mind that. But if ah get ter know French, ah can 'ave dealings wi' t' great folk, an' maybe benefit from it."

"Perhaps ah'll never be a foot serjeant," said Robert reflectively, "but ah mean to try."

III

The hauberks were finished by the end of the week, and the helmet would have been too, had not Robert delayed matters.

"Weer's that helmet?" said Brom.

"Ah finished it," said Robert, "but ah had ter tek it to t' leather shop so's they could mek a linin' for it."

Brom accepted this explanation without question and told Robert to get the handcart and return the hauberks.

It was always Robert who was sent to the castle because only he knew enough French to speak to the constable, should it be necessary, and though many of the foot serjeants were English, about half the men-at-arms were of Norman origin, and the knights were all of Norman origin. Toby followed him as usual, without being asked. As, of course, he believed it to be his duty to stick by his master.

The castle seemed busier than ever, and the guard had been doubled. There was no friendly greeting at the Outer Gate today, and the men-at-arms practicing at the pell seemed too busy to take notice of him.

Adam was sweating over his forge while his apprentice hammered at the anvil with a sense of urgency that was probably related to the pile of broken arms and armour that awaited their attention.

"Ah, at last!" said Adam, noticing his visitor. "Put 'em dahn o'er theer, an' tek these others."

Adam sorted out another four hauberks from the pile in the corner. and Robert stacked them on to the handcart. As he was tying them in place, Constable Heydon came into the forge and started talking to Adam in French. Robert pretended to concentrate on the knot he was tying, but he was all ears. His knowledge of French was still not good, but Adam spoke French poorly and Heydon had to speak slowly and in simple terms, so Robert managed to pick out the gist of what was said.

It seemed that Heydon was complaining about slow work. He had swords, daggers, lances, that needed repairing, arrow heads that needed making, and a hundred and one other things that needed repairing. Adam protested that he was doing his best, and blamed the delay on the slow work of the village blacksmith. Robert nearly intervened at this point, but he bit his lip and decided to keep quiet – he would learn more, that way.

Heydon went on to explain to Adam that the conference at Bath between King Stephen and the Empress Matilda had ended in bitterness and that they were going to fight it out. Sir William was building up his forces in support of

King Stephen, and Coningsburgh needed all the men it could get – and that meant more arms and armour. Adam asked if he could have another apprentice. Robert's ears pricked up at that – perhaps this was his chance to get into the castle, at least – but Heydon said they could not spare a single man. Instead, Adam was to send more work to the village.

Then it was over. Constable Heydon hurried off to deal with another problem, and Adam went back to his work. Robert bid him goodbye, called Toby, and began to push the overloaded handcart, his muscles bulging tight against his shirt. But he hardly noticed the physical extertion because his mind racing with the implications of what he had heard – was this his chance? Had the time come to present himself as a foot-serjeant? He was so absorbed that he didn't hear a little voice calling from somewhere high above.

"À bientôt, Toby!"

But Toby did. He stopped and barked up at the keep. Robert stopped then, and looked up, and there, 60ft above him, was Isabel leaning dangerously out of the solar window with Bijou tucked under her left arm. With her right hand she was waving Bijou's paw.

Robert was not sure whether it would be right for him, a humble peasant, to wave back at a princess, so he solved the problem by picking up Toby and waving his paw, too. Isabel leaned out even further and called, "La prochaine fois, venez jouer!"

Robert knew that she wasn't asking *him* to come and play, but Toby. He didn't know how to reply, but Toby answered for him with an enthusiastic, "Wuff, wuff!" to which Bijou replied, "Ouf, ouf!" At the same moment a black-clad arm caught Isabel by the waist and pulled her away from the window.

But beautiful princesses and doggy friendships were the furthest things from Robert's mind as he dragged the heavy cart up the steep hill from the castle to the smithy. He was making a plan which he intended to carry out the very next day.

It was a glorious morning in midsummer. The guard on the Outer Gatehouse had just changed, and the replacement foot serjeant was rubbing away the sleep that still bleared his eyes. Looking up again he was surprised to see a strange-looking soldier walking towards him. The soldier had all the right appurtenances, but somehow seemed all wrong. The helmet was banded and riveted, the jupon, coloured with the wrong shades of blue and gold. The spear was too short, and the spearhead too small. The sword stuck through the man's belt, had no scabbard, and looked suspiciously like a large kitchen knife. Even more puzzling was the little black dog that trailed behind him. Nevertheless, the man was tall and strong, and his powerful musculature could be guessed from the size of his course hessian sleeves and the breadth of his chest.

The guard decided to take no chances and rang the warning bell. Immediately another guard appeared and they levelled their halberds at the strange visitor. The first foot-serjeant gave the challenge: "Halt, who goes there?"

"Hey up, Dirk. It's me Robert."

Dirk looked disbelievingly at him, so Robert took off his helmet.

"Does tha recognize me nah?"

Dirk did, but was still uneasy. "What's all this abaht, then?" he said, nodding to indicate the armour.

"Ah've come ter offer mesen as a foot-serjeant."

The two guards looked at each other for a moment, then burst into hearty laughter. Tom felt embarrassed and blushed like a girl. Now that he was standing a few yards away from two real foot-serjeants he could guess how foolish he looked. Nevertheless, he was determined to see it through. After all, was not Sir William desperate to built up his army?

"Well?" said Robert, "Ah tha guin' ter let me in?"

"Aye," said Tom, "if tha promises not ter tek t' castle."

This quip doubled them up again, and they were only called to their senses when the Gatekeeper appeared and said, "Nah then, lads. What's all this about?"

They told him, and perhaps the Gatekeeper was a more serious-minded man, or perhaps he bit his lip very hard, but he didn't laugh. He simply said, "Well then, Robert, tha'd best report to Serjeant Dufton. 'Ees o'er theer watchin' t' squires at t' pell."

Robert followed his directions, and as soon as the squires at the pell caught sight of him they all stopped and one of them laughed. Serjeant Dufton turned on them at once. "Back to the pell, or I'll use you as one!" Then he turned to Robert, looked him up and down contemptuously, and said, "Well?"

"Ah've heard that me lord is recruitin' foot serjeants," said Robert.

"That's true," said Serjeant Dufton. "What about it?"

"Well, ah want ter join up."

Serjeant Dufton did know whether to be angry or amused, but he realized that, if he made a joke of it, the squires at the pell would stop again, so he decided to be angry.

"You come here dressed in a toy soldiers' outfit and expect to be taken on as a foot serjeant! A foot serjeant has to provide all his own kit, and has to have years of training – and another thing, he has to know a bit o' French."

"This is my kit," said Robert, looking down at his jupon, "et je parle un peu de Français."

"Very well, show me your sword."

Robert, feeling very foolish now, took out his kitchen knife. It was the best, biggest and sharpest knife from his mother's kitchen – but it was no sword. Serjeant Dufton sighed, made a grimace, and then said, "Take that jupon off

– they're the wrong colours anyway. The blue is too dark, and the gold is too yellow."

Robert took off his jupon to reveal the patched, rusted, mail underneath. Not only was it in poor condition, it had no sleeves and was much too short. The sight was too much for the squires at the pell to resist. They had stopped practicing and had edged closer without Serjeant Dufton noticing.

"And as for this," continued Serjeant Dufton. He took Robert's spear and snapped it easily across his knee. "As I thought. It's softwood! A spear shaft should be made of yew! And another thing…" He tried to kick Toby away, but Toby dodged him. "We don't want dogs on the training ground!"

The squires burst out laughing the moment the spear snapped, and one of them called, "You should have broken it over his head!"

Serjeant Dufton also snapped and it was a lot less funny than the breaking of the spear. "Back to the pell, you lot, and you'll find yourselves on double duty from tonight!"

Then, turning back again, intending to dismiss Robert without hurting his feelings too much, he found that it was too late. Robert, overcome with humiliation, had fled.

IV

When Robert got back to the forge, he rolled up his armour in an old blanket and consigned it to the back of a deep and dark cupboard.

"Weer's tha been, lad?" said Brom.

"To t' castle," said Robert, and before Brom could ask him why, he added quickly, "Constable Heydon said there's a lot more work an' we're to work faster."

"Aye, well, ah'd better see abaht them new apprentices today. Nah, while I'm aht, ah want yer ter 'ave a gu at mekin' a 'elmet. Tha's 'alf done it already, an' they's wantin' six moor by next Friday."

Being entrusted with this difficult and important job went a long way towards restoring Robert's shattered self-confidence. He would rather be a foot-serjeant, but being a blacksmith was worth something after all. At this rate, it would not be long before he was a blacksmith too. He was already far ahead of the other apprentices.

He said nothing of his disappointment to Mildred, but kept his promise to teach her French, and in doing so, found that his own French was getting better and better. Now, when he went to the castle, he could talk to the Norman men-at-arms in French, and even Toby was beginning to bark in French with more of a "Ouf, ouf!" sound, which he copied from Bijou.

There was so much work, that Summer became Autumn, and Autumn became Winter with Robert hardly noticing. There were new arrivals at the castle each day, as Sir William built up his army, and more and more work for Brom. Robert no longer went to the castle with the handcart, but leading Dobbin and a large four-wheeled waggon.

It was a cold December, the more so it seemed to Robert because of the contrast with searing heat in the forge. The door stood open as always, and the gusts of cold wind were welcome, but when he stepped outside, the cold hit him like a fist, and on his walks to the castle he was chilled to the bone.

At the midday break on Christmas Eve, Mildred said, "You lot can get yersen's a round o' bread an' a bit o' cheese. Me an' Bessy's trimmin' up fer t' feast. An sure enough the back kitchen, the centre of the forge's social life, was already half covered in holly, ivy and other evergreens.

That evening, Brom brought out the cask of ale he had been saving for the occasion, and Mrs Smith proudly uncovered the goose that had been roasting on a spit over the fire for most of the afternoon. Several friends called in; the butcher, the baker, the candlestick maker, and somewhat more interesting to the apprentices than these portly burghers and their wives, their rosy-cheeked daughters dressed in their best.

They partook heartily of the Christmas feast – and a feast of plenty it was, all good things being in abundance in the smithy because of the excess of work. After the feast, the miller struck up on the rebec, and the revelers formed couples for dancing. Robert had hoped to dance with Marla, the miller's buxom daughter, but somehow he found himself partnered with Mildred.

"Ah know tha fancies Marla because she's got more up front than me," she said with her customary frankness. "But ah'll 'ave bigger ones than 'ers, one day. You'll see."

Robert wondered if he would see, and decided that he would like to.

The miller scraped his rebec faster and faster and the dancers whirled around the room more dizzily than ever. Toby was dancing too. Despite several attempts to shoo him into the back yard, he managed to sneak in again, and when he wasn't hunting for scraps under the table enjoyed getting under peoples' feet and tripping them up.

After several dances, each one faster than the other, the music stopped, and everybody was breathless and laughing.

"More ale!" called Brom, and his wife went round with the jug.

"More dancin'!" called Marla.

"A kiss!" whispered Mildred, glancing upwards. And sure enough, she had manouvred Robert just where she wanted him – under the mistletoe.

It was a long kiss – longer than an under-the-misletoe-kiss, but not so long that it attracted attention from the others.

"Don't get any ideas, mind," she warned Robert with an arch look. "Ah'm only 11, an' anyway, ah mean ter rise in t' world. Ah'm not throwin' mesen away on a Coningsburgh apprentice!"

A wuff from between his feet told Robert that Toby agreed. But before he could make his own reply, Marla had stolen him from Mildred, and Robert had the satisfaction of watching her well-developed boobies bounce as they danced the next dance together.

It was late in January that the vague rumours of war that had been circulating since the previous Summer were replaced by definite news. The news was that the Lord of the Honour of Conisbrough, Sir William De Warenne, had come in person to marshal his army. For months he had been with the king's party, first at Bath for the negotiations with the Empress Matilda, and then at his castle at Castle Acre near Kings Lynn. Now he arrived with his household knights, Sir Jerville Boswelle, and Sir Fulk Foljambe, their squires, and a personal guard of twenty men-at-arms.

Robert, as usual, was the first of the Conisbrough folk to hear about it on one of his visits to the castle. He also found out the reason from Serjeant Dufton: "Ranulf of Chester and William de Roumane rebelled against the king and, by a trick, captured the castle at Lincoln – and it would have to be by a trick, because that castle is twice as strong as this. Why? Because it's got two keeps – yes – two! Once inside they overpowered the king's guards and admitted Robert of Gloucester and his army. We're to march next week!"

Robert could not help himself. "Will yer tek me this time?" he blurted out.

"Wuff!" said Toby, as if to say, "Please."

Serjeant Dufton laughed. "Nay, lad. Soldiering is not for you, but I'll tell you what. We're going to need another blacksmith at the castle. Adam and his apprentice will go with us in the forge wagon. What do you say, lad?"

"But ah know nowt o' castle work," protested Robert.

"Why don't yer keep Adam's apprentice 'ere, an' let me gu in t' forge waggon."

Serjeant Dufton considered the idea for a moment, then replied, "Very well, if Adam is agreeable."

Robert was over to the Castle Forge in a moment. He gabbled his request without preamble, and while Adam, considered it in his slow way, his apprentice said, "Let Robert gu. Ah've no wish ter get cut ter pieces!"

And so it was decided. Brom was not pleased to lose his best apprentice, but knew that, when the army marched, the work coming into his forge would dwindle with a trickle.

"All reet, gu on then," he said in a reproving tone. "But dunna forget tha's still got three years apprenticeship ter serve, an' a want thee back." Then he added in a pleasanter tone, "So dunna get theesen killed."

Robert was ecstatic. He hurried to the deep, dark cupboard and pulled out his "toy soldier" armour. It wasn't much, but it would have to do. He was going into battle as a blacksmith's apprentice, but he intended to come out of it as a foot serjeant.

V

Meanwhile, in the Great Chamber of the round keep, a council of war was taking place. In the centre of the room was a round table, which was so old and battered that some had joked that it was the original round table used by King Arthur. Around the table sat Sir William and his knights, with their squires in attendance. Sir William was a young man of only 22. He was tall, handsome, good humoured, and his bright eyes burned with the enthusiasm of youth. It was clear that he saw the coming conflict as a chance to prove himself to his king and thank him for his recent gift of Thetford, the second most important town in Norfolk. To his right sat Sir Richard Heydon, Constable of the Castle. He had a thin, bony appearance, and the reputation of being something of a tyrant behind my lord's back, though he was obsequious enough in his presence. Sir Jerville Boswelle was another young knight, who shared De Warenne's idealism. One day he would inherit a manor in Kent, but its revenues were small, and he too welcomed the chance of winning the king's favour. The fourth knight was Sir Fulk Foljambe, a grizzled veteran of many campaigns who had buried his idealism with his best friend in a mass grave after the Battle of Alençon.

"Now, Heydon," began De Warenne, "what men have we at Coningsburgh?"

The Constable stroked his beard as he considered the question, then began hesitantly to enumerate my lord's forces: "200 men-at-arms and 300 foot serjeants, more or less."

"What do you mean, 'more or less'?" said De Warenne.

"Men are coming in all the time," explained the Constable. "Only yesterday we had 20 archers arrive from your domain in Wales."

"Very well, go on."

"60 garrison guards, the 20 archers I mentioned just now, and an assortment of squires, pages, fletchers, farriers, blacksmiths, grooms and assorted varlets – around 600 souls all told is my guess."

De Warenne nodded with satisfaction. "There are another 400 at Sandal, 500 at Castle Acre, 300 at Lewes, and… as for Reigate, I cannot say, but that is a worthy army to deploy in support of the king."

Sir Jerville and Sir Fulk nodded their agreement, but Sir Richard looked uncertain. "My lord," he said hesitantly. "Who will guard the castle when we are gone?"

"We will use the Castlegardurn men for that," said De Warenne. "How many are there, Heydon?"

"What are Castlegardurn men?" said Sir Jerville, who had heard the word before but had no clear idea of its meaning.

Constable Heydon answered in a condescending tone as though he were a schoolmaster teaching a boy a lesson he ought to have learned long ago.

"Castlegurdurn is a feudal obligation by which those who hold lands from my lord pay for it with military service. If they do not wish to serve in person, or send substitutes, they can pay a tax called quit-rent. But in times of need, my lord can insist on service in person."

"But they are a sorry lot," added Sir Fulk, with a gruff chuckle. "Fat burghers who have never picked up a sword in their lives! They're unsoldierly to say the least, armed with rusty old helms and ill-fitting hauberks, with their pot-bellies hanging out below."

"They'll do," said De Warenne. "I don't want to deplete my army for the sake of providing a guard. The Empress Matilda will have a lot to do before she gets as far as Coningsburgh!"

At last the day came when Robert said farewell to his friends at the forge, and with his pack on his back – a heavy pack for, in addition to food and clothing, it contained his hauberk and helmet – set out for the castle.

He had only just set foot through the gate when he found himself in the middle of a disorganized crowd of Castlegardurn men. They were milling around, complaining and looking confused, because neither they nor Sir Fulk could understand each other. Sir Fulk spoke English, but he had only been at Conisbrough for a week and as far as he was concerned the local dialect might have been the language of the Medes and Persians. As soon as the Castlegardurn men saw Robert, they seized on him as an interpreter, and having a voice at last, became even more vociferous.

Godfrey of Top Field pushed his way forward and said, "Who's goin' ter milk me cows while ah'm standin' around on a tower doin' nowt?"

"Wot! Tha never milks thy own cows, does tha?" said Simpkin the Miller. "An't tha got milkmaids to do that for thee?"

"Aye, an' proper pack of lazy hussies they is! If ah'm not there, standin' o'er em, nowt ud get done and t' cows ud bust their udders!"

Robert translated to Fulk, who reacted indignantly, shouting in loud English that was clear enough, even if strongly accented. "Shut that talk! You're a soldier now! Stand up straight and try to look like one!"

"But me cows…"

This didn't need translating. It was simple enough, but it was also disobeying a direct order.

"Serjeant! Discipline that man!" said Sir Fulk to the nearest foot serjeant. The foot serjeant grabbed the unfortunate farmer with his mailed gauntlet and dragged him away, protesting at the top of his voice about his cows.

"Right," said Sir Fulk. "That man is going to spend the night under the same roof as my lord, though in the lowest room – the dungeon. Anybody else who speaks out of turn will join him!"

That did the trick, and the Castlegardurn men settled down into a resentful silence.

"Now," said Sir Fulk. "I'm going to allocate your duties…"

Other than the Castlegardurn men, who had been dragged away from their comfortable homes by their feudal obligations, everyone else in the castle, from the lowest varlet to my lord himself, was brimming with enthusiasm. It seemed that everyone was running hither and thither in a hopeless chaos, but from that chaos a kind of order was emerging. By late morning, a train of waggons and a row of packhorses were standing ready in the Outer Bailey loaded with everything that the Council of War thought they would need: arms, armour, clothing, food, ale, wine, kitchen utensils, tents, blankets, and a thousands other odds and ends. A whole wagon held a miniature smithy, and this was where Robert was to fight his war. He jumped up beside Adam, flung his kit bag into the back, and said, with an enthusiasm that was not reflected in his new master's eyes, "When do we start?"

He was answered by the sound of a trumpet, announcing the Lord of the Honour of Coningsburgh, who rode to the head of the great army assembled in the Outer Bailey and gave the signal to march. Piers, his squire, rode proudly beside him, carrying his helmet and his lance. Trumpets sounded again, and under the direction of the knights, three cheers were raised for Earl De Warenne and another three for King Stephen. As De Warenne rode out of the gatehouse he was followed by the men-at-arms, then the foot-soldiers, then the archers, and finally the baggage train and the vast assortment of squires, pages, fletchers, and farriers – and, of course, Adam and Robert in their forge waggon. Toby tried to follow, but he was 'arrested' at the gate by the guard on duty, who happened to be Godfrey of Top Field.

VI

It was the first day of February when the army set out on their march south. They were joined by the Sandal men on the Old North Road who swelled the army to well over a thousand men, so that from the vanguard to the rearguard was a matter of miles. They camped at Lindsey and the following morning, early, marched on to Lincoln. The castle was already under siege by the king's army, and De Warenne joined his forces with the king's. The Castle Acre and Lewes contingents were already there, though there was no sign of the men from Reigate.

The baggage train formed up with the king's baggage train to the west of the armies, and Adam and Robert began the work of setting up the forge. Already men were coming to them with requests to repair equipment that had broken on the march, or to shoe horses, or sharpen their swords.

Robert felt a such a thrill as he surveyed the scene that he could hardly concentrate on his work. There to the east were the twin keeps of Lincoln Castle, and spreading out on either side, the curtain wall and massive gatehouse of the city. The walls were lined with garrison guards and archers, and the king's archers were ranged in front of them, kneeling behind their pavise shields. The archers of both sides exchanged shots, though with no visible effect from where Robert was standing. The king's army was still manouvring, and from time to time, a body of knights would gallop from one part of the battlefield to another.

"Robert!"

It was Adam, calling Robert back to his duties.

"'T' buckle on this 'ere 'arness 'as broke. It needs welding. See to it, an' stop moonin' arahnd!"

Robert did as he was told, but his thoughts were on the battle and that kit bag full of armour he had brought with him. His plan was to wait for the right moment, put the armour on, join the battle, and prove himself. Not for one moment did he think that he might die instead.

De Warenne, meanwhile, had just heard bad news. His Reigate men were delayed, and would not be there until the following day.

"It'll all be over by then!" he fumed.

But Sir Fulk galloped up to him with news that was much worse. "The Empress's army is just to the west of us, and it is huge. There are Robert of Gloucester's men, those of Ranulf, Earl of Chester and those disinherited by King Stephen – and what is worse, there's a mass of Welshmen led by Madog ap Maredudd, Lord of Powys, and Cadwaladr ap Gruffydd."

De Warenne forgot the Reigate men in the urgency of

the moment, and gave orders to wheel his army about to face the new threat. King Stephen, and his leading nobles, William of Ypres, Gilbert of Hertford and Hugh Bigod did the same.

The first that Robert knew about it was when Sir Jerville galloped up and ordered the baggage train to move north.

"But, beggin' yer pardon, sire," protested Adam, "we've just set the forge up…"

"Do as you are ordered, or the enemy will save me the trouble of thrashing you!" And without further explanation, he galloped off.

Grumbling and groaning, Adam slowly set about obeying the order.

"An how does 'ee expect me ter tek dahn a red 'ot forge? It'll tek 'ours fer it ter cool!"

But the other waggons were beginning to move, and a moment later, a group of fletchers ran through the makeshift smithy as though the devil himself were after them. "Run for your life!" one of them called.

Belatedly, Adam caught on. "Ne'er mind t'forge," he said to Robert. "Throw what yer can into t' waggon and let's get aht o' 'ere!"

Robert needed no telling, though it wasn't fear he felt, but rather a rising sense of excitement. Perhaps his moment was not far away.

The king, seeing that the armies were roughly equal in size, took the decision to offer battle rather than retreat. He saw from their banners that the disinherited knights, led by Baldwin de Redvers were in the centre. On one flank was Ranulf of Chester with his Welsh auxiliaries, and on the other Robert of Gloucester, the leader of the Empress's army.

The king disposed his forces rather differently. He placed himself at the back of the field and fought on foot, surrounded by his household troops, also on foot. In front was his cavalry, the knights and men-at-arms brought by his earls including De Warenne.

There was a sound of trumpets and the disinherited charged those who had it all. Perhaps it was their superior numbers, perhaps it was their superior skill, but more probably it was the anger they felt at having being disinherited from their lands and titles by the usurper king. Whatever it was, it carried the charge, and they crashed into the king's men like a stampede of bulls, their lances like horns, piercing and killing everything in front of them. One by one the king's men went down in screams of agony, lances through their bodies, or swords hacking off arms and legs. Blood flowed until the grass was slippery, and those who were unhorsed were trampled to death.

The Coningsburgh men fought bravely. De Warenne, with Piers beside him as shieldbearer, charged the disinherited with such fury that he disinherited more than a few of their lives. Fulk was close beside him. He had lost his lance, but swung his sword with such force that he decapitated the knight in front of him and was drenched in a shower of the man's blood. Sir Jerville had also lost his lance, and was swinging his sword with a speed that spoke of panic, but at least served to keep him alive.

William of Ypres had greater success on the left flank against the poorly armed Welsh auxiliaries, but Ranulf of Chester, who stood out from the mass in his bright armour undimmed by surcoat or jupon, turned the tide of battle with a well-organised charge of fully armoured knights.

Sir William, who was a veteran of many battles, judged that it was now impossible to assist the king, and that it was better to make an organized retreat than throw away the lives of his men to no purpose. Accordingly, he led his men out of the field, heading north to avoid the river. Seeing this, many other knights joined the retreat, and with William of Ypres men hard on their heels, the retreat soon turned into a rout.

With fewer and fewer men beside him, De Warenne felt

that he had no choice. "Retreat! Retreat!" he yelled to his men. They couldn't hear him, of course, but they saw him turn his horse, and were not slow to follow him.

The baggage train had managed to get safely out of the way, but was in chaos. The forge waggon lost a wheel on a rutted road, and Adam was not slow to abandon the wagon. He unharnessed one of the horses, and called to Robert, "Come on, lad! Tek t' other 'oss an' let's get aht o' 'ere! It looks like our side is losin'!"

Robert did indeed unharness the other horse, but he had no intention of following Adam. He took his kit bag out of the waggon and put on the hauberk, helmet and jupon that had occasioned such hilarity only six months before. There was a sword in the waggon that had been brought for sharpening, so he tucked that into his belt, and picked up a spear that someone had dropped in their panic. Then he jumped up on the horse and turned its head towards the action.

One after another the fleeing men hurried past him in the opposite direction; knights, men-at-arms, squires, foot serjeants, and every other type of combatant, some on horseback, others on foot, but all with only one aim in mind – to save themselves.

As he got nearer to the main battle he could see that it was going badly for the king. On every quarter around him there was a flashing like fire from the meeting of swords and helmets, and a terrific noise of clashing, crashing, shouting and screaming, which the city walls re-echoed. Most of the Empress's army were attacking the king, with the aim of capturing him, but others were pursuing the fleeing knights. With horses spurred on, they slew some, wounded some, and made others their prisoners, hoping for a generous ransom.

Robert slowed his pace as doubt entered his mind. What should he do now? If he pressed on, would he not also end up as a prisoner? And then he caught a glimpse of the De Warenne's blue and gold chequers. There! There was his lord attended by his squire and some of his men-at-arms — and close behind them was a party of disinherited knights. They were gaining. One of them caught up with one of the men-at-arms and hacked him down. Three others surrounded another man-at-arms and took him prisoner. The rest of De Warenne's men spurred their horses for all they were worth, and managed to draw ahead of their pursuers — but De Warenne himself was left behind. A moment laster, the Coningsburgh men were flashing past Robert, and among them he recognized Piers, De Warenne's squire, whose duty it was to stand or fall with his master.

This was the chance he had been waiting for. He lowered his spear, wishing that it was a proper lance, and charged at the knight immediately behind De Warenne. The knight was focussed on his prey and little expected to be attacked from the front, so Robert's spear was through him before he even saw it. He fell to the ground, where he writhed in helpless agony in a pool of blood, taking the spear with him. Robert drew his sword and charged for the next man, who took one look at this hulking Fury and decided it wasn't worth it. He turned his horse and beat a hasty retreat to the safety of his own lines.

Seeing that there was no more opposition, Robert wheeled his horse, caught up with De Warenne, and rode beside him.

"Merci mille fois," said De Warenne, gasping for breath after his exertion. "May I know to whom I owe my life?"

"It's Robert, sire," replied Robert in French, grinning all over his face. "I'm the blacksmith's apprentice."

For a while, De Warenne said nothing as he was unnerved and exhausted by his brush with the Grim Reaper. He rode on, hard, glancing behind every now and again to see if he was safe, and sometimes at the man who rode by his side, no doubt trying to understand the significance of the strangely coloured jupon. After a while De Warenne slowed his pace, and asked the question that had been in his mind.

"And what is a blacksmith doing in battle?"

"I want to be a foot serjeant, sire. So I thought I'd try to prove myself."

"You've done more than prove yourself, Robert. Now where's that God-cursed squire of mine? Piers!" he shouted.

But there was no sign of him.

"He ran away when I needed him most," growled De Warenne. "So, I'll tell you what. You can be my squire until we get back to Coningsburgh."

All the Coningsburgh men headed for the Old North Road which took them directly away from the battle, and led, straight as a die, to the safety of the walls of Coningsburgh Castle.

One by one, De Warenne's men-at arms – those that had survived the battle – came together. There was Sir Fulk, who had done good service with his lance and sword, and was soaked in blood – luckily not his own. Sir Jerville had survived too, and looked white-faced and shaken after the experience of his first battle. A little later, Piers rode up to join them, but De Warenne dismissed him scathingly.

"Call yourself a squire! You left me to my fate. I would be dead or a prisoner if it were not for Robert, here!"

"I'm sorry my lord," said Piers. "It won't happen again."

"You're right about that," said De Warenne, "Get back to your father's castle in Witham, and tell him you're a good-for-nothing coward!"

That outburst seemed to do De Warenne good, for he softened a little, and added, "Well, on second thoughts, you can stay at Conignsburgh, but you can squire for somebody else. Robert here is my squire, now."

Perhaps De Warenne had reflected that Piers was not

the only one who had let down his lord and master that day. Had not De Warenne himself, and Sir Fulk and Sir Jerville, along with William of Ypres and a host of others, fled when they should have stayed to fight for their king?

They heard of the king's fate even before they got back to Conisbrough, when one of the last knights to escape, Sir Gilbert de Grant, told them in dramatic terms how the battle ended:

"The king fought bravely to the end slaying his attackers with his immense battle-axe, but there were too many of them. In the end, the king's battle-axe was broken; but even then he held them off for a while with his sword, until that, too, was broken. On seeing this, William de Keynes rushed upon the king, and seizing him by the helmet, cried, 'Hither, all of you, come hither! I have taken the king!' Robert of Gloucester took his surrender, and the king is now a prisoner of the Empress."

That brought gloom indeed to De Warenne. He felt that he had let his king down, and also felt in great peril himself. His one thought was to get back to Coningsburgh and garrison it with the utmost strength.

As for Robert, he cared little about the complicated politics behind it all. He knew nothing of the reasons behind the war; that King Stephen was a usurper; that the Enpress Matilda was fighting for her hereditary right. Nor did he give any thought to where his loyalty should lay – to the king or to his lord, or even to his apprenticeship master, Brom. De Warenne had twice called him his squire, and the second time, it sounded as though he had meant it. So, though Robert could hardly credit his luck, his plan, which had been a long shot at best, had actually worked, and now he was a squire. That would mean that one day he would be a foot serjeant at least, and perhaps even a man-at arms.

4. TOURNAMENT!

Three chapters of my book, The Abduction of Lady Alice, consist of a description of a tournament. The tournament takes place at Pontefract Castle, but a contingent of Coningsburgh knights plays an honourable part, not to mention the archer, David of Doncaster. This tournament actually took place (in 1313), though much of the descriptive detail is fictional. Some of it from my own imagination, and some of it inspired by the tournament in Sir Walter Scott's Ivanhoe

I

Spring seemed long in coming, but when it did come, it brought with it an additional promise; the Earl of Lancaster had announced that he was holding a tournament at Pontefract Castle. The tournament was both a celebration of the pardon, and a preparation for the coming campaign in Scotland. After all, tournaments were in essence, bloodless (relatively) battles, and the best preparation for war that could be devised.

Soon after the announcement of the tournament, Eland received a message from De Warenne about his intended preparations. He would bring knights from his castles in Reigate and Castle Acre, and together with the knights of Coningsburgh, Sandal and Wakefield, would form a party to compete in the tournament. Of course, all the squires would attend, and many of the men-at-arms, who would be needed to guard the De Warenne enclosure.

Never was such excitement felt at Coningsburgh! The bailey rang with noise of blacksmiths mending armour and sharpening swords. The tilting yard resounded with noise of lance on quintain and baton on pell. Serjeant Greathead allocated the squires to the special service of one of the three knights (usually they served in rotation in between their many other duties). Myles was allocated to Eland, with Will as his second squire, and Gerard and Tom were allocated to serve San Martin. Eubulo was allocated as second squire to De Warenne. He was pleased about this, for he was beginning to fear that his earlier service had been forgotten, however, he did not look forward to the prospect of having to work with Esteven.

The party that set out for Pomfret was enormous. Even though Coningsburgh only fielded three knights, their train was stretched over several miles of road. There were two destriers for each knight, as well as hacks for travelling, then there were their supplies of arms, armour and lances. As they travelled, they were joined by contingents from De Warenne's other possessions; Sandal and Wakefield in the north and Reigate and Castle Acre from the south, as well as a small group from his Welsh domains. They were also joined by other parties travelling in the same direction – the Tickhill Castle contingent was particularly large, consisting of eight knights, and hundreds of retainers, and they all brought squires, pages, men-at-arms, archers, farriers, armourers, and numerous-hangers-on. In addition to the official parties were huge crowds of common folk who were determined to make a holiday of it.

The setting for the tournament was a large natural amphitheatre about a mile north of the Castle and All Saint's Church. The ground sloped gradually down on all sides to a level bottom where the palisades had been set up. Despite the distance, the castle's size and magnificence made a great impression on Eubulo. He had seen many castles, but nothing quite like this. In extent it was at least twice the size of Coningsburgh. The keep, which was higher and wider, was of an unusual multi-lobed design which gave it something of a French appearance, like the illustrations he had seen in Lady Joan's Book of Hours.

The palisades had been enclosed by a wicket fence which was guarded by men-at-arms. There were two entrances, one to the south, which contained the pavilions of Lancaster's champions, and one to the north for the pavilions of the challengers. A further large space to the north was reserved for the tents and waggons of their supporters. At either side of the palisades, wooden terraces had been constructed for the comfort and convenience of the nobility. The central part of the southern terrace included a raised tier which was roofed, and decorated with multi-coloured hangings and pennants bearing Lancaster's arms: the arms of the kingdom, differenced by a label France of three points. This raised tier was intended for the earl, his wife, and his immediate family. Those of lower rank had to make themselves comfortable as best as they could on either side of the terraces, the common folk being relegated to the wide grassy spaces outside the enclosure.

Eubulo surveyed these arrangements with enthusiasm until he was recalled to his duty by an order from De Warenne, "Help me into this doublet," he said. The next hour was spent lacing the pieces of armour into place one by one, beginning with the sabatons and ending with the great helm. De Warenne walked up and down a few times to test the fit of the many different plates, and asked Eubulo and Esteven to make several adjustments. Then, seeming satisfied, he took off the great helm and gratefully gulped a lungful of fresh air.

"I am ready," said De Warenne, "so let us watch the lords and ladies arrive."

The Earl of Lancaster's party rode to the terraces, dismounted and made their way to their places in the highest tier. Lancaster sat in a throne-like chair specially prepared for him, and his wife sat on a similar, though smaller, throne by his side. Eubulo couldn't take his eyes of her.

"You have noticed the fair Alice, I see," laughed De Warenne. "She is Alice de Laci, countess of Lincoln, Salisbury, Lancaster, Leicester and Derby, and as far above you as is the sun."

The sun was a good metaphor, for the Lady Alice was not only far above him, but had golden hair, bright eyes, and a radiant personality. In addition, she glittered with ornaments. A large, jewelled cross hung at her breast, though his eyes were soon distracted by the globes of ivory which it nestled between. A gold coronet circled her brow, and her Lincoln scarlet gown was embroidered with gold thread.

A trumpet sounded and Lancaster's steward, Michael de Meldon, acting as marshal, announced that the tournament was about to begin and read out the rules: "First, my lord of Lancaster presents five champions who are ready to take on all comers. They are: Sir Humphrey de Bohun, Sir Henry de Laci, Sir Hugh de Quarmby, Sir Robert Beaumont, and Sir Ralph Exley of Exley Hall and Siddal in Southowram. Second: that arms of courtesy shall be used – you shall save your points and edges for the Scots! Third, that the prize shall be the Sword of Honour – that sword which is displayed in my lord Lancaster's pavilion, and that the winner shall have the privilege of naming the Queen of Beauty."

The rules being read, the marshal gave the field to the

heralds, and already there was a crowd of knights at the barrier, eager to make a challenge, San Martin foremost among them. That wily old knight had been heard to say: "I am not rich, like Sir John, and can ill afford to forfeit my horse and armour. So my plan is to challenge Sir Henry. He is the weakest of the champions, and I have a good chance of winning. The price of his horse and armour will be very welcome."

He was not the only knight eager to challenge Sir Henry, who was the oldest of the knights, and past his best. His daughter, Lady Alice, had pleaded with him not to take part, but he would hear none of it. His head was still full of the victories of his youth, and he had not allowed himself to notice that his prowess was fading. Others had noticed it, however, and were keen to win an easy ransom.

Sir Baldwin Picott of Tickhill beat Sir Richard to Sir Henry's pavilion, where he touched his shield with his lance point. The two combatants made their way to opposites ends of the lists and prepared to charge.

Trumpets sound. The herald cries: "Laissez aller!" and the two opponents spur their horses. They meet with a resounding crash. The horses rear and buck, and both riders fight for balance, but Sir Henry is the better horseman and brings his horse under control at the same moment that Sir Baldwin hits the ground in a cloud of dust. Trumpets sound again, and the herald proclaims Sir Henry the victor.

Other bouts are fought, but Sir Richard is waiting for the next round, and this time he is successful in challenging Sir Henry. Flushed with confidence, Sir Henry is perhaps not as careful as he was in his first bout, whereas Sir Richard knows that to lose his horse and armour would be disaster. He double checks every strap and buckle of his horse's harness and his own armour, and finally mounts into the saddle where he sits with grim determination. His face cannot be seen for it is hidden by his battered great helm, but his mood can be judged by the way he hunkers down on his horse. On his feet, San Martin is short and awkward, but on his horse, his deformed posture allows him to crouch down so that almost all of him is behind his shield and his centre of gravity is low; he therefore makes a formidable opponent.

Trumpets sound, and the challengers speed towards each other. Sir Richard watches his lance tip, keeping it as straight and true as possible, then he switches his attention to his opponent's shield which bears the arms: Or, a lion rampant, purpure. He aims for the lion's heart. His aim is true, but so is Sir Henry's. The shock nearly unseats him, but his hunchbacked posture, low in the saddle, tells in his favour, and it is Sir Henry who is unseated. Moments later, Sir Henry's squire is helping him to his feet. He heaves off his helm, and his genial features are covered in sweat. But he is wearing a broad grin. He has proved himself in the lists yet again. He has won a victory, and suffered an honourable defeat – and as for the ransom of his horse and armour, it is a mere nothing by comparison. Sir Richard, too, is happy. The ransom that Sir Henry must pay to redeem his horse and armour will keep him in coin for many a long day.

Not all the knights perform so well. Sir William of Wakefield, riding against Sir Humphrey de Bohun, cannot even keep his lance straight. It swings awkwardly as he begins his charge, and goes so far to the left that it strikes Sir Piers sideways across the chest. The impact knocks the lance out of Sir William's grasp, and the joust is declared attaint, that is to say, in breach of the rules, and Sir William's horse and armour are forfeit.

As the day wore on, Lancaster's champions achieved their vow of fighting five challengers, or were defeated, as de Laci had been. The mighty Sir Humphrey, Earl of Pembroke, known as 'the oak' by virtue of his enormous bulk and strength has done particularly well, and looks set to win the contest. However, despite the fact that his bulk and strength makes him difficult to unseat, he is not the best of Lancaster's team. That honour goes to Sir Ralph Exley, but he has not fought a single bout due to his formidable reputation. De Warenne, who had been watching the proceedings with the eagle eye of the expert, suddenly announced: "It is time to show them what a real knight can do! Esteven, my helm! Eubulo, my lance! Farrier, my horse!"

He spurred his horse forward to the far end of the lists and called in a loud voice: "Exley! I challenge you!"

Eubulo noticed De Warenne's grim expression, and remembered that his father, the 6th Earl, had been killed in just such a joust. No doubt, Sir John was thinking of that too – a joust was no knightly game for him, but a necessary trial of physical and mental strength, the latter being to overcome his deepest fear, of dying like his father, not in battle, but in a mere game of war. Exley, who had been waiting impatiently for someone to challenge him, nodded eagerly and waved to his squires to prepare him.

When both knights were ready and facing each other from the opposite ends of the lists. The heralds sounded the trumpets and the two great destriers leapt forward, De Warenne's covered with a barding of Chequy Or and Azure, Exley's in a barding of Argent, with martlets, gules. Both were highly skilled in the joust, Exley, bolstered by his formidable reputation, and De Warenne by his grim determination to avoid his father's fate.

Their meeting resounded like a thunderclap as lance met shield and shield met lance without attaint – in other words, straight and strong, so strong that De Warenne's lance splintered. Exley's, however, went through De Warenne's shield and threw him off his horse. He landed face down in the dust with a great crash and clatter of steel plate. Eubulo and Esteven rushed to help him, and found him stunned, but able to get to his feet. They were helping to walk back to his pavilion when Eubulo noticed that Sir John's left pauldron had been torn away, and that there was a gash in the mail underneath. Blood poured from the gash, soaking the gold and blue jupon. He cried out at once: "Marshal, Exley's lance was sharp! Sir John is wounded! Come and see for yourself!"

The Marshal rode over, dismounted, and inspected the wound. Then he turned to Exley, "What have you to say to this, my lord?"

Exley was dismissive. "The foil came of my lance, that is all. Anyway, there's no harm done. It is only a scratch."

"He should be disqualified!" cried Eubulo.

"I will consult my lord Lancaster," said the Marshal.

The verdict, that it was an accident, was only to be expected, as Exley was Lancaster's first knight. The herald announced the verdict to the excited crowd: "The wound to Lord De Warenne was an accident due to a defective foil, and no blame therefore attaches to Lord Exley. Therefore Exley is adjudged to be the victor!'

A loud cheer was raised by Lancaster's men, though there were many cries of "Shame!" – and not just from the Coningsburgh contingent.

Exley ignored these, and rode up and down the lists with his lance in the air exulting in his victory. The herald cried the words he would have said for himself: "Is there another challenger?"

There were no takers. The suspicion of foul play had deterred anyone else from coming forward, even to challenge the lesser knights among Lancaster's champions. The herald cried again: "Dare any man challenge Sir Ralph Exley?"

As there was still no reply, the herald looked to Lancaster, who nodded with satisfaction, and was about to declare Exley the winner of the Sword of Honour, when a voice cried out: "Wait! I will challenge him!"

Everyone looked to see who it was, and there, at the far end of the lists, was Eland, still dressed in travelling clothes.

"Gramercy, my lord," he said, addressing Lancaster, "there was an important matter to be dealt with at Coningsburgh – but enough of that. I am here now. Just grant me the time to arm."

Lancaster looked at Exley, who nodded his agreement.

"Granted," said Lancaster, and both men went to their pavilions to get ready.

Eubulo hurried to warn Eland. "Sir John!" he gasped. "He has just wounded my lord Warenne with a sharp lance, and Lancaster let him get away with it!"

"Well, we'll ask the Marshal to check his lance this time," said Eland. "Now where are my squires?"

"But, my lord..."

"Oh, I know what you are going to say. I know I spend too much time in the office and not enough in the tilting yard..."

"I have never seen you in the tilting yard," interrupted Eubulo.

"...but I can still hold a steady lance – and then, there is the lady..."

"Lady?" said Eubulo, thinking of some noble dame who had given him her favour .

"Lady Luck!" laughed Eland. "She was ever on my side, and I trust she will not desert me today!"

Meanwhile, Exley had quaffed a cup of wine to refresh himself, and having poured another, walked over to Eland's pavilion.

"You are wasting your time, Eland – not to mention throwing away your valuable horse and armour. I have just beaten Coningsburgh's best knight!"

"I heard differently," said Eland, "and consider the word 'cheated' more appropriate than 'beaten'. Well, this time, I will ask the Marshal to make sure your lance is properly foiled – then we shall see. In the meantime, I advise you to change your horse."

Exley threw down his half empty wine cup in defiance

and strode back to his pavilion. He immediately mounted the same horse that he had just used, as if to say, I can beat you easily, even with a tired mount! Then his squire handed him a new lance, which both the Marshal, and Myles, who was squiring for Eland that day, checked carefully.

Whether it was Exley's arrogance, or Eland's Luck, that made him use the tired horse, it told against him in the encounter that followed. His lacklustre charge caused his lance to glance harmlessly against Eland's shield, while Eland charged hard, and as he had said to Eubulo, held a steady lance, with the result that Exley was swept from his saddle. He found his feet quickly and drew his sword. Seeing this, Eland also drew his sword, but the Marshal rode between them, reminding them that such a form of combat was forbidden by the rules.

"You have robbed me of my just reward!" growled Exley.

"It was your own arrogance that was to blame," responded Eland. "I warned you to use a fresh horse!"

"We shall meet again," said Exley, his eyes flashing with anger, "and next time there will be none to separate us!"

"I will look forward to it," said Eland.

Lancaster had watched the encounter with a range of emotions beginning with smug satisfaction and ending with disgust, but he had no choice but to put on a courteous face and present the Sword of Honour to Sir John Eland.

A fanfare sounded as he received the prize, and a mighty cheer went up from the crowd, most of whom were delighted to see the double-dealing Exley get his come-uppance, but the loudest shouts of all were: "Coningsburgh! Coningsburgh!" For, despite De Warenne's defeat, the Coningsburgh men had come out the best: San Martin had beat De Laci, and Eland had beat Exley, and won the Sword of Honour.

II

Sir John had also won the privilege of naming the Queen of Beauty. This was no easy decision, politics being what they were. His first thought was that it was his duty, as De Warren's liege man, to choose his wife, Lady Joan – but then, Sir John was not on good terms with his wife. Another consideration was that his own daughter, Rowena, would be hoping that he would choose her. In the end he decided to keep faith with the spirit of the title, and to choose the most beautiful lady at the tournament, and there was only one choice – the Lady Alice, Lancaster's wife. His liege lord might be put out, and his daughter might be disappointed, but everyone else in the vast crowd would surely agree with him, as she was by far the most beautiful woman at the tournament, though if the truth be told, Lady Joan could have matched her beauty had it not been overcast by the dark cloud of her sorrow.

The Marshal placed a crown of roses (with their thorns removed) on the tip of Sir John's lance, and he rode to the gallery to present it to her. This was not an easy manouvre, but it was presumed that the knight whose horsemanship was good enough to win the joust would be skilled enough to avoid spearing the Queen of Beauty. Despite the fact that his body was tense, with his knees gripping his charger, and his arm straining to steady the heavy lance, Sir John carried it off with an air of graceful ease. Lady Alice took the crown, and placed it over her gold coronet, while the crowd roared their appreciation. Even Lancaster smiled. There was not much love lost between him and the Lady Alice, their situation being a surprisingly similar to that of De Warenne and Lady Joan. Nevertheless, the compliment was not lost on him.

When evening came, the tournament gradually turned into a fair. Hawkers and peddlers moved among the crowd selling their wares, and jugglers and jesters tried to earn a few coins by entertaining them. In De Warenne's pavilion, a table was spread for the entertainment of his knights and squires, while the Coningsburgh men-at-arms, armourers and farriers sat down at a long trestle table outside.

Sir John Eland was the hero of the hour, and the talk was of his courage in challenging the best of Lancaster's champions and his skill in defeating him.

"His arrogance defeated him," said Sir John, modestly.

"Arrogant or not, it still took a steady lance to bring him down," said De Warenne.

"He didn't take his defeat too kindly," said San Martin.

"That was the second time he broke the rules of chivalry," said De Warenne, ruefully rubbing his bandaged shoulder.

"Chivalry is a game for dreamers," said San Martin, "and while you are playing your games, Lancaster is pursuing his ambition with deadly intent. That lance was no accident, my lord. It was meant to kill you – you know why."

"Because I deserted the Ordainers and went over to the king – well, that business with Gaveston sickened me. I realized then that Lancaster is ruthless, and he will not stop until he has taken the crown for himself!"

"Do you mean to fight in the mêlée tomorrow, Sir John?" asked Eubulo, who had been listening intently to this discussion.

"Of course. Why shouldn't I?"

"Because you will be an easy target," said San Martin.

"Then I will rely on you to protect me," he said, and with a large gesture that included them all, he continued, "but we will let tomorrow take care of itself. It has been a good day for Coningsburgh. No more of this gloom and doom. Let's refill our cups and celebrate!"

Soon the pavilion was filled with happy laughter and the excited chatter of the squires who were looking forward to playing a more active part the following day. Squires were not allowed to fight in the mêlée, but they had to help their knights with their horses and weapons, and carry them off the field if they were wounded.

"I thought we were going to miss it," said Will, as he recounted his experiences of that morning. "Sir John insisted that we punished the miller before we set off."

"The miller?" said Esteven. "Why, what did he do?"

"Stole the corn meant for the castle – well some of it."

"What did Eland do?"

"Hahaha – threw him in the dungeon!"

Eubulo was enjoying the conversation when it was interrupted by a visitor to the pavilion, one of Lancaster's pages. A moment later, De Warenne said, "Eubulo, you're wanted at the castle. The Lady Alice has heard of your skill on the lute and wants you to sing to her!"

"That's right. Go and entertain the ladies, while we men plan for the mêlée," said Esteven, who couldn't resist a dig at his old rival.

Eubulo said nothing but did not try to hide his disappointment. He would much rather have stayed there carousing with his friends. There were times when he regretted that he ever learned to play the lute.

That feeling was much mitigated when he saw Lady Alice again. In the soft torchlight of the Great Solar in Pomfret keep, she looked even more beautiful than ever. Lady Joan was with her, along with the old duenna, and two maidservants, one of whom Eubulo recognized as Mildred.

It was another magnificent chamber, though it had none of the heavy majesty of the Great Hall. Instead, the emphasis was on elegance and comfort. The walls had been partly wainscoted and the stonework above the wainscot was softened with silk hangings and tapestries. It was like walking into an Arthurian Romance, especially by comparison with the mud, horse manure, sweat and stench of the lists.

"I am sorry to take you away from your revels," said

Lady Alice, "but my friend, Lady Joan, tells me that you are an accomplished troubadour."

"It is my pleasure," said Eubulo, executing his best courtly bow, "but you flatter me. I play a little, it is true, but surely there are better minstrels at the tournament than me!"

"Ah! But we prefer a gentleman troubadour!" said Lady Alice archly.

Eubulo bowed again. Then he settled down to tune the lute that Lady Alice handed to him. When he was satisfied he said, "What would you like me to play?"

"A love song," she said with girlish giggle. Eubulo thought for a moment, then began:

Les tres doulx yeux du viaire madame
Me font souvent rire et joye mener
Son doulx maintieng et son tres doulx parler
M'ont mis ans feu d'amours droit en la flamme.

(The sweetest eyes of my true lady
Often make me laugh and be happy,
Her sweet bearing and sweetest speech
Have set me in the fire of love, right in the flames.)

While he was playing he was conscious that Lady Alice was watching him intently, though when his eyes met hers, she looked away again quickly. Lady Joan's eyes were downcast throughout the whole performance.

That evening, Eubulo sung several songs, was offered a glass of wine and some sweetmeats, and sent away only when the page came with a message for Lady Alice.

"You must come again. The page will show you out," she said as he bowed his farewell.

The page led him along a series of gloomy passages and staircases, lit only by smoky cressets, and some not lit at all, until at last they came to the great hall. They were just about to descend the grand staircase to the main entrance, when Eubulo caught sight of Esteven.

"I thought you men were planning for the mêlée," said Eubulo ironically.

For a moment, Esteven was too surprised to reply, then he collected himself, and said, "Indeed, and some negotiations with my lord Lancaster have been necessary."

"Well, I shall be there to assist Sir John, so I hope you'll tell me what I need to know," said Eubulo, though he had no doubt that Esteven would deliberately leave him in the dark to make him look a fool.

In the event Eubulo was not there to assist Sir John. He had risen at dawn with the other squires to get De Warenne ready for the mêlée. The Coningsburgh knights were discussing tactics, and in particular, how to ensure that Exley could be prevented from using the confusion of the mêlée as a cover for another attempt to kill De Warenne.

"I want my men at arms near at hand," said De Warenne. "Esteven, keep close to me, so that you can fetch help if necessary. Eubulo, your job will be to watch Exley and let me know if he does anything suspicious."

But no sooner had De Warenne given him these instructions, that he was called to the castle by Lancaster.

"Damn the man!" said De Warenne. "He knows very well what he's doing – depriving me of my best squire!"

Eubulo grinned and glanced meaningfully at Esteven, who pretended that he hadn't heard, but his grin was short lived when it dawned on him that if they kept him for long he would miss the mêlée, the part of the tournament he had most been looking forward to.

This time he found Lady Alice alone, except for her maidservant. She seemed surprised to see him. "I thought you would be fighting in the mêlée," she said.

"Sir John said that you had sent for me," said Eubulo.

"Not I," said Alice, "but since you are here, you can entertain me."

Sir John's words sprang to mind, and he felt a strong urge to turn on his heels and go straight back to the Coningsburgh pavilion, however, an inner voice told him that to do so would be a breach of the code of chivalry. He therefore overcame the impulse and went to get the lute.

But Lady Alice stopped him. "No," she said, "save that for this evening. I'd like you to read to me." She gave him a beautifully bound book. "This is my favourite. It is about King Arthur and was written by Chrétien de Troyes. You are a minstrel, so perhaps you have heard of him." Eubulo nodded. "I particularly like the story of Lancelot and Guenevere." She flicked through the pages, found the passage she liked, and said, "Start here."

Eubulo's mind was on other things, the mêlée that he was missing, but he did his best to enter into the spirit of the story and read well. After all, to be alone – almost – with Alice – would have been a dream come true at any other time.

One day there rode up to the Castle a band of horsemen sent by the King, to bring her to his Court, and at the head of them Sir Lancelot du Lake, friend of King Arthur, and winner of all the jousts and tournaments where Knights meet to gain honour. Day by day they rode together apart and he told her tales of gallant deeds done for love of beautiful ladies, and they passed under trees gay with the first green of spring, and over hyacinths covering the earth with sheets of blue, till at sunset they drew rein before the silken pavilion, with the banner of Uther Pendragon floating on the top. And Guenevere's heart went out to Lancelot before she knew.

Alice sighed. "I love those words: 'Guenevere's heart went out to Lancelot'. Ah! what it must be to feel true love!" She said these words more to herself than to Eubulo, and he wisely refrained from comment. After a moment she said, "Go on."

There was an interesting fight scene between the Knights of the Round Table and the men of Sir Meliagraunce, which must have called forth a wistful sigh from Eubulo, though he was not aware of it, because Alice interrupted: "I see you are yearning to get back to the tournament! Well, I won't keep you long. Just read one more scene, here."

Alice came very close as she leaned over the book to point out the words, so close that he could smell her perfume. Her delicate finger traced the line, and he felt the urge to put his hand on hers, but quickly suppressed it. He was but a humble squire after all, and Alice was a great lady. He read on:

'Oh, mercy,' cried Sir Lancelot, 'I may not suffer longer this shame and noise! For better were death at once than to endure this pain.' Then he took the Queen in his arms and kissed her, and said, 'Most noble Christian Queen, I beseech you, as you have ever been my special good lady, and I at all times your true poor Knight, and as I never failed you in right or in wrong, since the first day that King Arthur made me Knight, that you will pray for my soul, if I be here slain.'

Lady Alice sighed again. "The perfect expression of amour courtois! See how much Lancelot loves her! And yet he is content to love her from afar – despite that stolen kiss – and always remains loyal to his king."

She looked thoughtfully at Eubulo, then said with an arch smile, "Tell me, Eubulo, who is the object of your amour courtois?"

Eubulo felt uncomfortable. He did not want to confess his interest in Lady Joan, because he already felt that was a thing of the past. It had been eclipsed, and it was the bright sun that shone before him now that had done the damage – and yet, he didn't dare to suggest that perhaps she was the object of his devotion.

"I am but a poor squire..." he began.

Alice laughed. "Even a poor squire can love from afar – and anyway, poor squires turn into knights as readily as frogs into princes in children's tales."

Not if they don't get a chance to prove their mettle, thought Eubulo.

"Ha! I can see what you are thinking!" laughed Alice. "So I will let you go. I see that you prefer breaking heads to breaking hearts!"

What did Lady Alice mean by those last words – whose heart was he breaking? Or was it just an elegant play on words? By the time Eubulo reached the area marked out for the tournament, he found that his mental state was reversed. Instead of being in a lady's solar, dreaming of being at the tournament, he was at the tournament dreaming of being in a lady's solar.

It was in this absent-minded state that he rode onto the field, making for group of knights who were wheeling around a horse barded with blue and gold. The arms proclaimed it to be one of the Coningsburgh knights, and the crest on the helmet meant it was probably De Warenne.

It was only when he saw Eland galloping towards the group shouting, "Coningsburgh, to me!" that he realised that something was wrong. All other considerations vanished in an instant as his attention focused on the press around De Warenne. He spurred his horse to get there as quickly as he could, but hesitated to draw his sword – squires were not supposed to fight in the melee, only to help their knights.

Everything seemed to happen very quickly. Exley, with the help of several more of Lancaster's knights, among them Quarmby and Sir Humphrey, managed to unhorse De Warenne. Exley jumped to the ground, and drew his sword. De Warenne, lying helpless on his back, raised his hand and said, "I yield!" but Exley took no notice and raised his sword as if to strike. Just then, Eland crashed through the press, rode up behind Exley, and struck him across the back with such force that he staggered and fell. It was lucky for Exley that the contest was fought with blunt swords, or he would have been a dead man.

At that moment, Esteven arrived, and seeing that Lancaster's men were now ganging up on Eland, shouted, "Marshal! Marshal!" but, not surprisingly, the Marshal was nowhere to be seen. Eubulo was also surprised that Esteven had not been by Sir John's side to help and protect him, as he had been commanded to do. Where had he been and what had he been doing?

San Martin had also responded to Eland's cry for help, and arrived at the press just as Eubulo himself arrived. Now there were sufficient Coningsburgh men to ensure fair play, even in the absence of the Marshal. Eland dismounted in time to catch Exley before he had recovered himself, and with his sword to his throat, demanded his surrender.

"Curse you! Eland! I'll get even for this!" snarled Exley.

"Say the word!" demanded Eland.

"I yield," spat Exley.

De Warenne scrambled to his feet, and would have attacked Exley had not San Martin held him back. "That man tried to kill me!" he yelled.

It was then that the Marshal arrived, and of course, he dismissed any accusations of foul play. "Tempers get heated," he said, "that's what I'm here for."

"But you weren't here," Eland pointed out.

"Well, I am here now, and from what I have heard, Sir John yielded to Exley and so his horse and arms are forfeit."

"And Exley yielded to me," said Eland, "so his horse

and arms, and any horse and arms that he has captured are forfeit to me – and I hereby return Sir John's possessions."

"You took unfair advantage!" protested Quarmby.

"Tempers get heated," said Eland, throwing the Marshal's words at him. "But whatever happened, you all heard Exley yield."

"You attacked me from behind," growled Exley. "Next time we will meet face to face!"

The Marshal intervened to separate the two parties, insisting that De Warenne's men retire to one side of the field and Exley's men to the other. Tempers were getting heated in other parts of the battlefield, too, so the Marshal decided that it was a good time to bring the proceedings to a close. The herald sounded the trumpet, and one by one, the knights returned to the gallery to hear how the battle had been judged. It was no surprise to the Coningsburgh men that Lancaster declared one of his own party to be the winner. In the confusion of the mêlée it is difficult to be sure which knight has performed the best, therefore it would have been difficult to quarrel with Lancaster's decision, though most of the watchers would probably have chosen Eland.

Nevertheless, the honour of the Coningsburgh party had been saved once again, and the celebration in De Warenne's pavilion was even more raucous than the night before. Eubulo was in high spirits too, for he felt that his honour had been upheld by the fact that he had returned in time to support Sir John in his hour of need. True, he had done nothing, but he was there as a witness, and if things had gone badly wrong, he had been ready to use his sword.

So it was not without mixed feelings that Eubulo saw Lancaster's page bring a message to De Warenne. He knew what it was – he was to go to entertain the ladies again, but this time, though he would miss carousing with his friends, he felt himself looking forward to another session with Lady Alice, and – emboldened as he was by the events of the day and a few pints of good English ale – he would not be so shy. Indeed, he resolved that he would find a way to declare to her that she was the object of his amour courtois.

Once again Eubulo found Lady Alice alone, and could not help wondering if it was by accident or design. However, it was not long before they were joined by an old duenna – it seemed that every fair lady had one of these dragons to guard her – and for a moment, Eubulo was daunted, and his intention of declaring his love would have been forgotten, except that Alice, when she came near him to request a song, added, "Don't mind her, she's as deaf as a doorpost."

Eubulo decided on a song with which he could discreetly plead his love. While he sang, he gazed into the deep blue heavens of Alice's eyes, and for the first time, he forgot that she was Lady Alice de Laci, Countess of Lincoln, Countess of Salisbury, and the Earl of Lancaster's wife, and saw her as just another woman, although a very special one to him – the woman he loved.

> *Je me recommende humblement*
> *a vous en plorant tendrement*
> *que de moy ayez souvenanche*
> *m'amour la plus doulche de franche*
> *l'ordre de mon avanchement.*
>
> *(I humbly recommend myself*
> *To you while begging tenderly*
> *That you would keep me in mind*
> *And my love, the sweetest in France,*
> *The means of my advancement.)*

When he came to the end of his song, Alice poured him a cup of wine – and did her hand tremble as she poured? Eubulo thought so. She gave him the cup and said in a low voice, "Do you know now whom you admire?"

Eubulo was still too shy to speak his answer, but the wine had made him too bold to miss the opportunity. So he took up his lute, and sang

C'est vous que j'adore.
J'aime personne plus.
Vous êtes l'ange de mon coeur;
Votre image est toujours dans mes yeux.

(It is you whom I love.
I love nobody more.
You are the angel of my heart;
Your image is always in my eyes.)

It was the creativity of Bacchus that had inspired him, for he knew no song with these words, but he made one up on the spur of the moment and sang it as though it had been composed by one of the great French troubadours.

Eubulo's heart was beating faster than it had done in the mêlée, and he had even less idea what to do about it. He wanted to lay himself at her feet, tell her he loved her more than anything else in the whole world, but that he was not worthy of her. He was not even a knight and so could not wear her favour.

She seemed to read his thoughts, and said tenderly, "You will be a knight one day – and then... and then… ah! But even then you must love me from afar, as Sir Lancelot did with Guenevere."

Eubulo wanted to remind her that Sir Lancelot had stolen a kiss, but had not the courage to say it. How strange that a young man, who, only hours before, would have risked life and limb in defence of his lord, lacked the courage to speak a few words to a fair lady! He wondered at his cowardice and was haunted by the old saying about faint hearts and fair ladies.

The evening went on in this way until the torches guttered low in their sockets. That woke the old duenna up, and with mutterings of how late it was, she attempted to shoo Eubulo from the solar. "Just one last song," pleaded Alice. In a moment of inspiration he chose:

Adieu, mon amour et ma maitresse.
Il faut quitter dès ce soir.
Adieu, ma belle maitresse,
Adieu, non, au revoir!

(Farewell, my love and my mistress.
It is necessary to leave you this evening.
Farewell, my beautiful mistress,
Farewell — until we meet again!)

III

By the time he got back to the camp, everyone was sleeping the drugged sleep of the tired and inebriate. He found a place among the squires and settled down too, though he thought it would be impossible for him to sleep, his heart was too full, and his mind kept repeating the words that Alice had said to him. In his imagination he kissed her, embraced her — and more, and soon he was asleep and dreaming, and her hot little hand on his arm turned out to be Myles' rough grasp as he shook him awake.

"Come on!" he said, "You'll miss the archery competition!"

The prize for the archery competition was a silver arrow — a much coveted prize, as it would set up a poor man for life. The competition centered around three Pomfret men who said they would prove that the crossbow was superior to the longbow. They were led by Lancaster's chief crossbowman, Fulk de Burgh. Favourite among the challengers was David of Doncaster, well known as the best bowman of the castle garrison. This time the knights were spectators, because, though they all learned to use the bow or the crossbow, the real experts were the men-at-arms, and the common folk, many of whom practised daily, building up great strength and accuracy. The three Coningsburgh knights, and their squires, therefore, were seated in a gallery not far from Lancaster's, and not far from the butts. San Martin was not too happy about this. "What if Lancaster's next plan is to dispatch you with a stray shot?" he said to De Warenne. Eland, however, was more complacent. "A stray shot in the opposite direction to the butts would look very suspicious. No, I think we'll be safe enough."

At the sound of a trumpet, the competition began. Archery was a popular sport in those days, so it was a long time before the lesser contenders were eliminated. At last it came down to Fulk and David. As they were both expert shots, the Marshal set the butt back from 100 yards to 150 yards.

"This will see you off!" said Fulk as he bent over with his foot in the stirrup to wind his windlass. Then he chose a quarel with great care to ensure that it was straight and true, and laid it in the groove. He aimed carefully, aiming slightly high to allow for the trajectory of the long shot, and slightly to the left to compensate for the slight breeze, then he pressed the push lever. "Thwack!" the quarel hit the white bull's eye, just off centre.

The crowd gasped in admiration, all except the Coningsburgh contingent who sighed with despair. Then there was silence again as David of Doncaster stepped up to the mark. He raised his bow and drew the string back to his ear, then paused for a moment as he sensed the wind and judged the trajectory. The arrow was loosed with the characteristic "twang" of the longbow, and landed with a louder "thud", also in the white bull's eye, and also slightly off centre.

There was a shout of approval from the crowd.

"Set back the butt!" called the Marshal, and the butt was moved to 200 yards – a very long shot indeed. Fulk was a very long time in setting up his short, but it proved to be time well spent, for his quarel sped straight and true to the very centre of the white bull's eye.

"That's it!" he said, "I've won! It's impossible to beat that!"

"True," said David, "but I can match it!"

"How! My quarel is dead centre! You are just wasting time. Concede the victory!"

David's reply was to take his position at the mark and draw his bow. Once again, he paused to feel his target, though taking no longer than before, and then loosed. He aimed the arrow on a high trajectory to cover the great distance – something that was very hard to judge – but he judged it right, for the arrow fell in exactly the same spot as the quarel, though at a steep angle, gouged it out, and stood there, quivering in the exact centre of the butt.

There was an enthusiastic roar from the crowd, who had never seen such shooting.

"It's my turn to claim victory!" said David, turning to the Marshall, but the Marshall judged the honours even and ordered the butt to be set back to 250 yards. There was a gasp from the crowd. This was an unprecedented distance, and now the butt seemed so far away that it was a mere dot in the distance.

Fulk shot again and hit the butt – way off centre, it is true, but at that distance it was a great achievement even to hit it. Then David stepped up to the mark and shot with the same confidence as before. A distant thud announced that he, too, had struck the butt, but it was only when the Marshal went to inspect it and cried out: "Bull's eye!" that it was certain who had won.

Moments later, David was standing before Lancaster

waiting to receive the silver arrow – though 'arrow' was a misnomer. In order to save on the precious silver, Lancaster had ordered a silver quarel to be made, and a small one at that. However, instead of presenting the silver quarel, Lancaster cried out: "Arrest this man!" and before anyone knew what was happening, two men-at-arms had stepped up to the gallery and seized David by the arms.

"What have I done!" he cried.

"Any man who can shoot that well must be Robert Hood. Well, Robert, at last I have you!"

"I am David of Doncaster!" expostulated David. "Ask any man here! Ask my lord De Warenne!"

"Ha! David of Doncaster, you say. A very good disguise! No doubt you have been fooling these innocent people for years! Take him away!"

Just then, De Warenne intervened. "What he says is true, Lancaster. This man is David of Doncaster, and one of my garrison. Please release him."

"What! Release the notorious Robert Hood! Never! If he is whom you say, it will have to be proved in court. Now, away with him!"

De Warenne made an angry motion towards Lancaster, well aware that he was doing this to provoke him, but Eland grabbed his arm and hissed in his ear: "Careful! He knows what he is doing. The accusation is nonsense, of course, but it would be a mistake to make a scene here. We can speak up for David at the proper time."

That being settled, Lancaster stood up and announced: "It seems that the winner of the archery competition is the notorious Robert Hood. He is now under arrest. Therefore, by default, the winner is Fulk De Burgh, and I have great pleasure in presenting him with this silver quarel."

The shouts of anger and disbelief from the Coningsburgh crowd were drowned by the general applause, as most people had no way of knowing that Lancaster's words were not true. But despite the disgust at the unfair treatment of one of their number, De Warenne's people were not displeased with their success at the tournament, and it was a happy crowd that wended their way home that afternoon.

5. RICHARD OF CONISBROUGH

Richard of Conisbrough was born in Conisbrough Castle only a few hundred yards from my family home in Castle Avenue. Of all the great noblemen who owned Conisbrough Castle, he was the one who spent most time there – even if the reason was lack of money. It is also likely that he was referred to as 'Conisbrough', it being contemporary practice to refer to noblemen by their titles. For these reasons, he is more fully 'Conisbrough' than any other historical figure associated with the town. part of his story was told by Shakespeare, and so I decided that the most appropriate form for a retelling of his story was a play, from which the following is an extract.

ACT IV, SCENE 2

The Great Hall at Conisbrough Castle. CAMBRIDGE is celebrating the birth of his son, Richard. He is attended by PETER, but we can't see them. We see only the lower table with SERJEANT GOODLAD, TOM, DICK and HARRY.

TOM
Why, ah've not seen such revelry as this since we were in Denmark.

DICK
Nor I, ever at Conisbrough.

HARRY
Well, 'tis the old Conisbrough custom called 'wettin' t'bairn's 'ead'. It's good to see one o' these trumped up Norman lords followin' t' old customs.

TOM
Norman? 'Ees as English as you are!

DICK
Ah'm Welsh. Well me dad is.

TOM
We're all mixed up now, anyway.

DICK
Mixed up or not. 'Is lot is till on top.

HARRY
On top! 'Ee's got no money. 'Ee must have visited t' Jews.

TOM
Well, ah dunna care weer 'ee gorrit from, ah'm goin' to wet me whistle good an' proper.

Enter SERJEANT GOODLAD.

SERJEANT GOODLAD
No you're not. You're on guard. Go to the gatehouse.

DICK
Dunna worry, Tom. We'll save yer a pottle!

SERJEANT GOODLAD

And you're on your usual beat – on top of the keep!

HARRY
Ah suppose ah'm on duty as well. Weer shall I go?

SERJEANT GOODLAD
Here, with me – I need somebody to share my revels!

TOM
'Arry 'as all t' luck!

DICK
T' biggest feast e'er seen in Coni, an' ah miss it!

SERJEANT GOODLAD
Don't fret. The quit-rent men will be here soon. They'll
relieve you.

TOM
If they turn aht at all.

DICK
If they dunna, ah'll gu an' drag 'em aht!

*CAMBRIDGE makes a speech offstage. The revellers at the lower
table listen and react appropriately.*

CAMBRIDGE
Lordynges, commoners, burghers and all,
I welcome you to share this happy day.
A son is born to us – we called him Richard,
and he will be the Duke of York one day.
Alas, my wife cannot share our rejoicing
and the old custom: 'Wetting the baby's head'.
The birth has left her weak. She is in bed
and is attended by the Conisbrough Leech,

who soon will have her on her feet again.
That small regret aside, rejoice with us,
because, for us poor mortals here on earth,
No greater joy can ever be our lot.
For in a son we are reborn again,
for in a son our name is carried on,
and in a son is immortality,
at least the only kind that man can know.
His birth has fired anew my old ambition,
to rise in wealth and honour. Thus, I vow
before you all that I will win for him
the lands and revenues that I am owed.
Now fill your pots and raise a toast with me
To Richard, Duke of York – third of that name!
May he, like me, win favour, friends and fame!

ALL
To Richard, Duke of York!

SCENE 3

Inside the solar at Conisbrough Castle. ANNE is sick with childbed fever, and CAMBRIDGE is at her side. PETER is in attendance.

PETER *(aside)*
In Conisbrough Church there is a stained glass window – and before you go looking for it, I am sorry to say that it was smashed by a Puritan and is no longer there – these religious zealots have got a lot to answer for, haven't they? Well, it shows a picture of a popular medieval image: the Wheel of Fortune. The rich and happy are at the top, the poor and unfortunate are at the bottom. The thing is, of course, that the wheel keeps turning, and I am sorry to say, that it turned for my lord Cambridge. At the feast of the Wetting of the Baby's Head, Cambridge was at the top, but here we are, only a few days after, and it looks as though

he's right at the bottom again.

CAMBRIDGE
You will get well, my love, and you will see
our little son stride nobly through the world.
I'll win my rightful place for him and you,
then we'll sit, two old and happy people,
in yonder window seat and gaze outside
over the verdant valley of the Don,
and laugh about our troubles. So get well!

ANNE
My lord, it is too late, my life is fading;
it's fragile candle flickers in the breeze
that soon will snuff it out, but oh, my lord,
I've had my happiness – you gave it to me.
You taught me how to love, and then our children
taught me again. I'm happy now, believe me,
and would be happier if you'll promise me
that you'll not grieve too much – better to raise
a chantry chapel in my memory –
but I am forgetting! – we're too poor!
I am so rich in love that worldly things
seem nothing. Well then, light a candle,
and think of me in heaven watching over you.
There's not much time. I pray thee, bring a priest –
but do not leave me without one last kiss!

Kisses her with tears in his eyes.

CAMBRIDGE
You cannot die! I'll bring the leech instead.

ANNE
It is no good, but, as you wish – bring both.

CAMBRIDGE
Peter, make haste, they're waiting just outside.

*Exit PETER. A moment later, he returns with the PRIEST and
the LEECH who motion to CAMBRIDGE and PETER to wait
outside. CAMBRIDGE paces up and down while PETER address
the audience.*

PETER
I can't say that I'm very religious. It's true that I go to the
castle chapel, the big one in the bailey, but only because my
lord makes me. But now I'm praying like the Apocalypse
had come. My lord has had his share of knocks, but if his
beloved wife dies, I dread to think how he will take it.

*He bows his head in prayer. A moment later, the LEECH and the
PRIEST emerge from the solar.*

LEECH
My lord, it was the dreaded childbed fever.
I did my best. I bled her like horse,
made her inhale hot fumes of Mercury
and drink a potion made of Belladonna.
But all to no avail. She writhed and screamed
then, weakening, she breathed her last and died.

PRIEST
But not before I gave her Final Unction
so now her soul is on its way to Heaven
Be comforted in that.

CAMBRIDGE
                    How speak of comfort?
My only love, my dearest Anne, is gone;
my best friend, comforter in all my trials,
support in sorrow, sharer of my joys,

mother of my children – how can I go on!

PRIEST
Be comforted – Our Lord succours our grief.
He died upon the cross for us, remember.
Then rose again, teaching us not to fear
th'inevitable end that comes to all.

CAMBRIDGE
I thank thee for thy spiritual counsel,
and thee, good Leech, I thank thee for thy skill.
Now leave me on my own to dwell upon
the question that is thrust upon my life –
how can I live without her?

PRIEST
                                        But alone?
It is not good to brood alone with grief.

CAMBRIDGE
I have my squire to tend to any needs.

PRIEST
Well, then, may God be with you in your loss.

Exeunt PRIEST and LEECH.

CAMBRIDGE
What is this cocktail burning in my breast?
Somehow my grief is boiling into rage,
making me rail against the universe –
now, I defy you – Stars, and cruel Fate,
that cast me from my mother's womb a bastard!
And you, King Henry! Who will not repay
my many services as they deserve.
Well, now I plan to rise by any means –

whether they're foul or fair, it matters not.
What, fair? Have I not tried throughout the years?
Defended Hereford against Glyndŵr,
Escorted Princess Philippa abroad –
and what have I to show for it – a knighthood
that's meaningless without grant of land;
a miserable £50 annuity,
and that not mine, but granted to my wife,
which now will stop. Fair means are foul
and foul are fair, and now will aid my purpose.
And I have other aid – I'm not alone.
Lord Scrope, I know, has reasons to rebel,
and Thomas Grey is just as poor as I.
I'll sound them out – but what shall be our cause?
Edmund de Mortimer's right to be king!
He was the heir presumptive to King Richard,
and is supported by some English nobles,
and Grey among them – why, he is his kinsman!
And mine too! Indeed, my brother-in-law!
We will proclaim him as the rightful king,
and when King Edmund sits upon the throne,
he will reward the men who put him there.
The highest honours, caracutes of land,
titles and privileges beyond count
the grateful king will heap upon our heads.
That settled, I'll sound out Lord Scrope and Grey.
and with their help I'll see a brighter day!

PETER *(aside)*

That was the straw that broke the camel's back. Look, Richard is a Conisbrough man, born and bred, so he can't be that bad, can he? He tried, he really did. He endured more than most men could endure, but when Fate poleaxed him with the death of his beloved Anne, I believe he went mad. So when we go into the final act, don't think too badly of him, will you?

In the last act, Richard gets involved in the Southampton Plot which was a plot to murder King Henry V and replace him with Edmund Mortimer. The plot was detected and Richard was executed. However, he was not 'attainted' so his son, Richard, was able to keep his lands and titles, and became Richard of York. One of Richard of York's sons went on to become King Edward IV, and another to become King Richard III.

6. DALRYMPLE'S DARK SECRET

I wanted to write something about Crookhill Hall, the fine old Georgian mansion in Crookhill Park which was demolished in 1968. However, the Woodyeare family, who lived there for several generations, led uneventful lives and it seemed unfair to make up a lurid tale about them. So for the purposes of this story, I invented a similar mansion called Clyfton Hall which I have placed near the modern village of Clifton. The other inspiration for my story was The Castle of Wolfenbach by Eliza Parsons, but as I wrote I found that ideas from Bluebeard and Jane Eyre found their way into the mix.

CHAPTER 1

"We are home at last," said Dalrymple, surveying his magnificent house and its extensive grounds with satisfaction.

It was not the first time that Augusta had visited Clyfton, but it was the first time she had heard it described as her home. Clyfton Hall was a large, handsome stone building, standing on rising ground, and backed by a ridge of high woody hills; and at that moment she felt that to be mistress of Clyfton was indeed something!

They descended the hill, crossed the bridge, and drove to the door; at which point the staff came out to greet them. Dalrymple handed Augusta down from the carriage, walked with her up the steps to the great front door, then swept her up in his arms and carried her over the threshold accompanied by a great cheer from the staff. Mr Wilkins, the butler, and Mrs Dufton, the housekeeper were waiting inside to greet them.

"Welcome home, sir, ma'am," said Wilkins.

"Welcome to Clyfton, ma'am," said Mrs Dufton with a curtsey.

Dalrymple acknowledged them absent-mindedly with a "Thank you, Wilkins; thank you Dufton," but Augusta was too busy trying to take in the scene before her. They were in the magnificent entrance hall, which of course she had seen before, but now, as mistress of the place, it wore a very different aspect. The family portraits ranged around the walls were her family portraits now, and their faces seem to look down at her from behind the gloom of the faded varnish quizzically, but not without an air of welcome. It would not be long before her portrait too, arm in arm with her beloved Dalrymple, would be hanging beside them.

"We will take some light refreshment, then I will show you over the house if that will not be too tiring for you. I am aware that you have seen it as a tourist, but there are some things that I particularly wish to point out."

Augusta was surprised that her husband could consider such a prospect tiring, but then she realised that he had been familiar with every corner of the house since he was a small boy. However, the prospect of seeing again the magnificent apartments of Clyfton as their mistress was a prospect of unalloyed delight.

Their refreshment over, Dalrymple led the way up the sweeping staircase to the first floor landing, and from thence into the Picture Gallery.

"This is the family with whom you have allied yourself," he said, moving his hand in a sweeping gesture to indicate the rows of family portraits, "and a more errant pack of rogues you will not find anywhere else in history!"

There was a deprecating irony in his words which told Augusta that, despite the questionable exploits of certain of his ancestors, he was inordinately proud of them.

"We are descended from the Fitzwilliam Dalrymple who fought alongside William the Conqueror at Hastings, but the first family portrait to have survived is this one from the time of Charles I. There he is: Henri Dalrymple – he was a cavalier, and of course, of the royalist party."

Henri Dalrymple was portrayed in the typical style of a cavalier of the time. The breastplate of the military man almost hidden under flowing robes of rich silk. He wore his wide-brimmed hat at a rakish angle, and stared down at them with the ghost of a smile on his lips, which hinted at his rollicking way of life. Augusta imagined she could see something of the face of her husband in the face of the cavalier, though the waxed moustache and elegant pointed beard made it hard to tell.

They passed by several other portraits with little comment, until Dalrymple came to a figure dressed in the fashion of the times of Queen Anne; that is to say, a powdered wig, a long coat with frogged button-holes, knee-breeches and buckled shoes.

"That's the black sheep of the family, or perhaps I should say the blackest of several black sheep. He is known as Dalrymple of the Hell Fire Club. They say he sold his soul to the Devil for 25 years of wild living. I don't know about that, but several dark deeds are held to his account. Rumour has it that he got a servant girl with child, and then murdered her to prevent it being found out. They say her ghost haunts the East Wing."

Augusta shuddered, and seeing this, Dalrymple added, "Oh, there are many strange tales told about Clyfton – but every old house has its share of tales. So if I were you, I wouldn't pay much attention to gossip from the servants quarters – that is, if you don't want to lay awake all night!"

They walked on a little further. "Ah! and here is my father! Old Mr Dalrymple, they called him in his latter years, but when this likeness was taken, he was not much older than I am now."

And there on the wall before her, Augusta saw a portrait that could have been Mr Dalrymple himself, were it not for the knee breeches and cocked hat. It showed him with his wife standing under one of the Clyfton elms with a shotgun under his arm, and his favourite retrievers beside him. In the background was a distant view of Clyfton Hall.

"It's by Gainsborough," he said, "who as you may know, was one of the finest artists of the time. I have heard that Sir Thomas Lawrence is the best portraitist just now, and as soon as I have time, I will see about commissioning him to paint a picture of you and me."

"I heard that Gainsborough was also famous for his landscapes," said Augusta.

"If it is landscapes you like, we must go to the far side of the gallery."

He led her along another wall and pointed out various landscapes by Poussin, Salvator Rosa, Gainsborough, and several lesser known artists. The last one was somewhat different to the others as it was done in pencil and wash, and had more the flavour of an architectural drawing, than a landscape painting.

"That is by a Mr Brown – 'Capability' Brown, as they called him. It is his design for the landscaping of the grounds of Clyfton. But enough of art! Let us inspect the main bedrooms."

Dalrymple led Augusta back onto the landing, and through another door. She found herself in an elegant high-ceilinged apartment lit by three tall windows with magnificent views of the park, which was not so different to the Capability Brown design, after all. An enormous bed stood to one side, and in the centre was a comfortable sofa, and several armchairs. An elegant Empire-style dressing table stood near the centre window. To the other side of the room were two doors.

"Dressing rooms," explained Dalrymple. "One for you and one for me."

He showed her into several more bedrooms, all equally elegant, though on a smaller scale. "These are the principle bedrooms of course. There are many more on the third floor and in the West Wing, so we have no difficulty accommodating any number of guests."

After that, Dalrymple showed her the library which contained a fine collection of books including some of the very first examples to leave Caxton's press. The dining hall, with its superb mahogany dining table of Chippendale's manufacture, and the ballroom. The furniture in latter was in dust sheets and the great chandelier had been lowered to the floor for cleaning.

"It is some while since it was used," explained Dalrymple. "But when you are settled in, and feel equal to it, I plan to host a ball for all the respectable families hereabouts – then you can meet our neighbours."

Augusta's imagination swept away the dust sheets and presented the ballroom in all its grandeur, overflowing with happy people, the great chandelier shining like the sun, the orchestra playing in the gallery, and herself the queen of the occasion!

"I will not trouble you with the North Wing. That is merely a series of apartments which I use for business purposes. There is the estate office, the servants' quarters, the kitchens – we can see all those on another occasion. But perhaps it will be worthwhile to have a quick look at the West Wing."

The West Wing was almost like a separate house, complete in itself with withdrawing room, dining room and bedrooms, all on a smaller scale than the main building.

When they returned to the Great Hall, Dalrymple said, "I have one more thing to show you, and I saved until last on purpose – as a surprise."

He led her through several smaller apartments towards the East end of the main building until at last they came to a large door, somewhat different to all the others in that it was finished in black Japan picked out with gold around the panelling. Dalrymple opened the door and Augusta gasped in amazement.

"Why, it is oriental!" she cried.

The walls were decorated in a style called Chinoiserie which depicted Chinese men and women in conical hats engaged in various activities in oriental landscapes. The furniture was all black Japan lined with gold. The chandelier was modelled on the shape of lotus leaves.

"I had it done for my sister's fifteenth birthday. She had seen the Pavilion at Brighton and admired it, so I had this done in the same style."

"I love it," said Augusta, "and if Henrietta does not object, I shall make regular use of it."

"Henrietta is presently living in London. She has her own establishment presided over by Colonel Shelby and Mrs Younge – and in any case, you are mistress of Clyfton now."

As they were leaving the room, Augusta noticed another door that they had not opened.

"Where does that lead to?" she asked.

It seemed that Dalrymple looked uncomfortable for a moment, but it passed quickly, and he answered with nonchalance, "That is the door to the East Wing, but it has been shut up these five years – and the place is still too big!"

"For one man and his sister, yes, but now that you have a wife and we plan to entertain, perhaps we should open it up again."

Dalrymple shook his head. "That would not be easy. The roof has leaked and the floors are rotten. I fear that anyone who tries to walk through the East Wing will very quickly find himself in the basement!"

After that, he changed the subject, and try as she might, Augusta could glean no more information about the mysterious East Wing."

CHAPTER 2

That night, as Augusta tried to make herself comfortable in the big bed (which was almost as big as the small bedroom in her old home at Oldcotes) she could not help but bring up the subject of the East Wing again.

"Fitzwilliam," she said, choosing her words carefully, "I could not help but notice that you seemed uncomfortable about the subject of the East Wing. Is there some dreadful secret attached to it?"

Dalrymple was silent.

"Some skeleton in the family cupboard, perhaps?" she added jokingly – but Dalrymple only frowned. Seeing this, Augusta's blood ran cold. Her pleasantry seemed to have touched a sensitive place.

"There is something," said Dalrymple in a solemn tone. "Something which I should have told you before we were married."

"It is nothing serious, I hope?" she said with alarm.

"No, not so serious, but – but it may change how you see me. I sincerely hope it does not."

"Well, what is it then? Speak! Put me out of my suspense!"

Dalrymple took a deep breath and said, "It is this – I have been married before."

Augusta rolled over on the bed and buried her face deep in the pillow, her feelings boiling with confusion.

"But why did not you tell me!" she cried.

"I tried! Believe me, I tried to introduce the subject several times, but it seemed that you always laughed at my hesitant start. And then in desperation I wrote a note and pushed it under your door — but it seems you did not receive it."

Augusta could not recall seeing a note. "Perhaps it went under the mat," she said.

Dalrymple sighed, the said earnestly: "I tried to tell you. I really did."

By now, Augusta had collected herself somewhat, and decided that perhaps her husband's revelation was not so bad after all, though that would depend on the circumstances.

"What happened to the lady?"

"We had only been married a year and she died of consumption."

"And what has that to do with the East Wing?"

"Well, you have seen the tower at the end of the wing — that was her favourite place. She had her private apartments there, and indeed, in that year, we spent more time in the East Wing than the rest of the house. When she died, I was heartbroken, and could not bear to touch any of her things, so I had the wing shut up."

Augusta had turned her face back into the pillow, and was sobbing quietly. It was the word 'heartbroken' that had upset her.

"But my dearest, loveliest Augusta," said Dalrymple, enfolding her in his arms, "you must understand that love is an unlimited quantity — like the sea. Just because I loved her once, does not mean I do not love you. Indeed, just now I love you more than anyone else in the whole world, and my only desire is to make you happy — that was why I was so afraid to tell you!"

He kissed her tears away as he said this, and she responded with fragile smile. "I understand, and I forgive you for not telling me sooner. I am sure I will feel better in the morning. I just need a little time to – take it in, that's all."

She was awoken next morning by the maid folding back the shutters, allowing a stream of clear January light to fall on the bed. She sat up and caught a glimpse of the rolling parkland, then turned to her husband who was still asleep beside her. She remembered all that he had done for her family – and for others too, even Captain Roustabout, who had done him such grievous wrong. He was a good man, and she should pity him for the suffering caused by his first wife's death, and drive away any childish jealousy – for she realised now that that was all it was. She had been upset the night before because she had felt jealous that her husband had once loved another. With a resolve to cast such unworthy feelings aside, she shook her husband, kissed him and said, "Time for breakfast."

After breakfast they decided to take a tour of the park. A bleak January sun was shining, but the air was cold, and Augusta shivered inside her pelisse, and snuggled her hands more deeply into her muff. They walked down to the stream, which had been widened by Capability Brown, but still looked entirely natural. They crossed the bridge, a beautiful three-arched construction made of mellow limestone, and then walked towards Clyfton woods which at that time of year were a cluster of bare tracery.

"You should see them in the full abundance of summer greenery!" said Dalrymple. "Now that is a sight worth seeing!"

"What is that tower rising though the trees over there," enquired Augusta. "It looks like a castle."

"Oh that!" he laughed. "That's a folly. There is only the one tower, and that is on a smaller scale than the real thing. It was built by my father at a time when the gothic was in fashion."

"How delightful," exclaimed Augusta. "Can we take a

closer look?"

"Are you sure you want to walk so far?" said Dalrymple. "It is a cold morning, and you must be chilled already. Your little nose is quite red."

"On the contrary," said Augusta, "I find the exercise most invigorating, though I confess my feet, and especially my toes, feel somewhat icy!"

"We will be quick then," said Dalrymple leading the way at a brisk pace.

The tower looked ancient. The stone was crumbling and it was entwined by ivy. "Are you sure you father built it?" said Augusta. "It looks hundreds of years old!"

"And yet it cannot be more than fifteen, for I can remember it being built. I was fourteen or fifteen at the time."

They walked through a door into a circular chamber around which a number of rustic seats had been arranged. "This is a pleasant place to take a what the French call a pique-nique, that is to say, a light open-air lunch. Though, of course, not at this time of year!"

"And where does that door lead to," said Augusta, pointing to an iron-studded door in a Romanesque archway.

"To the first floor and the battlements. Would you like to see? The view is magnificent."

The view was, indeed, magnificent, and despite the icy wind that penetrated her bonnet, Augusta wanted to linger and admire the view. The house itself was situated on rising ground on one side of the valley, the stream ran along the bottom, and the folly was situated on the rising ground on the opposite side, thus affording a panoramic view of the whole. Now Augusta could see Clyfton in all its glory. The elegant main building with its three stories of tall windows in the High Georgian style, and the two wings, each curving forwards and ending in a square tower. The park had been landscaped to look entirely natural, but groups of oaks and elms had been strategically placed by the hand of the master designer. It was the perfect picture of English landscape: rolling gently, articulated by groups of mighty trees, and set off by the stream with its elegant bridge which broadened to a large lake towards the West of the valley.

"All you can see belongs to Clyfton Hall," said Dalrymple, not without a touch of pride. "Every inharmonious object has been removed. There was once a village called Clyfton just there..." here he pointed to the East, "but my grandfather razed it to the ground as it spoiled the view from the house."

"But the inhabitants!" exclaimed Augusta.

Dalrymple laughed. "Don't worry! They were not razed to the ground with it! They were removed to the village of Edlington and provided with new cottages."

Augusta sat down on one of the rustic seats. "Ah! I could stay up here forever. Why, I shall come again tomorrow and bring Udolpho!"

"If that is your taste," said Dalrymple dismissively, "you will find it in the library. I am very much afraid that it is well stocked with the gothic. You will find all the usual offenders: Orphan of the Rhine, The Castle of Wolfenbach, Clermont. You can thank Henrietta for that."

"Well, sir, I have caught you out," teased Augusta. "How is it that you are so familiar with them?"

"Very well, I own it," laughed Dalrymple. "When the night is dark, and a storm is raging, there is nothing I like better than to curl up with a gothic novel."

"In the tower of the East Wing, perhaps?" suggested Augusta.

Dalrymple frowned and Augusta saw her mistake.

"I'm sorry. That place must have sad memories for you."

"Let us speak of it no more," said Dalrymple, his countenance clearing. "I want to show you the Secret Garden. We call it secret because it is a walled enclosure with formal gardens inside. You see, my mother didn't like

Mr Brown's natural landscaping and she insisted on keeping a formal garden. The compromise was to build a wall round it so that it wouldn't spoil the natural outlook. However, there is not much to see at this time of year, though at least you will find it sheltered from the wind. "

"Oh, I should love to see it!" cried Augusta.

CHAPTER 3

Several days passed pleasantly in this way with Augusta getting used to living her life on the grand scale of Clyfton. "Why," she commented to Mrs Dufton, "it takes me as almost long to walk from our bedroom to the breakfast parlour as it did to walk from Oldcotes to Roche Abbey!"

Every day there was a new delight to discover, for Clyfton was so big that it was not one house, but several houses, and not one park, but several parks and gardens. There was the vast orangery – a huge greenhouse that produced fresh produce all the year round, and which seemed to Augusta the closest she would ever get to walking in the jungles that she had read about; there was the lake, which had been created by damming the stream at the West end of the valley. It was said that there had been a village there before, and that on stormy nights the bells of the old church could be heard tolling in the depths of the waters; there was the gazebo – an elegant open structure which provided another place where pique-niques could be enjoyed once summer had come; there was the Mews – and extensive block of stables where Dalrymple's magnificent selection of horses were housed, along with several carriages of different types; and finally, there was the North Wing, the busiest part of the house, where all the affairs of the estate were managed, and where Dalrymple would repair for a few hours each day to meet with his tenant farmers, his lawyer and various tradesmen.

One day, Dalrymple spent longer than usual in his office in the North Wing, and appeared at dinner with a frown on his face.

"There is no help for it," he announced. "I must go to London. Why do I have to see to everything myself! Don't I pay Jaundice and Jaundice enough to take care of my affairs?"

Augusta looked at him with surprise.

"I'm sorry, my dear," he apologised. "I am ranting on. The long and short of it is that I must go to London tomorrow and meet with Lord Melbury and Mr Jaundice. It is about that woodland I wish to buy. You remember that I mentioned it to you; the one in Buxton. I shall stay with Colonel Shelby and my sister, and it will good to see her again. But nevertheless, I shall not linger, and shall be back before the week is out."

Augusta said that she would be sorry to be deprived of his company so soon after their marriage, but of course, she understood.

"Thank you my dear," he replied. "But we will speak no more of it just now. A gentleman never discusses business over dinner – and I see a fine bottle of Chablis before me!"

The following morning, after breakfast, Dalrymple ordered his carriage, then gave some instructions to Augusta.

"As I told you, I hope to be back within the week. But you need have no concern. You will find that everything here runs by itself – I have Mrs Dufton to thank for that. All you have to do is to tell her in the morning what meals you require, and she will see to everything else. But I will leave you these."

He gave her a large bunch of keys.

"These are keys to all the principal apartments. You will probably not need to use them, as Mrs Dufton has a duplicate of most of them. But, in the unlikely event that I should send to you for a paper from my study, she has no access to that, and this is the key."

He showed her a small key with a distinctive design on the end.

"Nor has she a key to the East Wing. This the one."

He showed her another, much larger key with an oriental motif – a yin-yang – on the end. "But," he added, "on no account must you go in there. You can go anywhere else in the house, but please do not go into the East Wing."

Augusta laughed. "Just like the Bluebeard story! But of course, I understand."

"I hate to leave you alone like this."

"I understand, dear. It is business."

"What I mean is, you should have a female companion. My former wife had such a one, and it is a comfort at times like this. Perhaps, like her, you have a sister who might fill the role; Millicant perhaps?"

Augusta shook her head. "Please spare me that! Listening to her perpetual sermonising would be worse than being in church all day. No, I am quite happy to keep my own company."

Dalrymple seemed satisfied with this reply and turned to go. Then he turned back again as something else occurred to him.

"Oh, one more thing," said he. "The weather is closing in, and we might have a storm tonight. So make sure the sashes are closed and the shutters drawn. Mrs Dufton will see to the house, but remember to close the ones in the bedroom. And now I must leave you – with a kiss."

With that, he kissed her goodbye, put on his greatcoat and went out to the carriage, John following him with his portmanteau.

CHAPTER 4

With Dalrymple gone, Augusta didn't know what to do with herself. She wandered through the Picture Gallery, shuddered at the portrait of Dalrymple of the Hell Fire Club, and remembered the story of the servant girl he had murdered haunting the East Wing. Perhaps that was another reason why her husband did not want her to go there. She walked around a little longer looking at the Dalrymples who had long since turned to dust, and trying to trace the likeness of her husband, then, tiring of this she remembered the gothic novels which he had said she would find in the library. She made her way downstairs, went into the library and soon found the shelf of novels which Henrietta had left behind. She reached down the first volume of the first three-volume novel that came to hand. It was *The Castle of Wolfenbach* by Eliza Parsons. She took it away with to the Withdrawing Room, and settling herself down on the couch, began to read. Before long, she was deeply engrossed in the story. After several pages, she came to the point where a servant, Bertha, explains to the Countess Matilda why the servants believe the castle to be haunted:

> *Count Wolfenbach married a very handsome lady at Vienna, and brought her here; it was then a beautiful place very unlike such as it be now; but howesomever they say he was very jealous and behaved very ill to the poor lady, and locked her up, and there she was brought to bed, and the child was taken from her, and so she died, and 'twas said that the child died, and so every body believes itis their ghosts that make such dismal noises in the castle.*

Augusta was struck for a moment by the passing similarity with Fitwilliam's story of a young wife who was brought home, only to die soon after – but there the similarity ended, and she reproached herself for making the comparison in the first place. She read on for a while, but found the author's style tedious, and the events she described highly improbably (Dear Reader! not unlike this poor narrative, I fear!), so she threw the book aside with disgust. Just then, the Laughton grandfather clock in the Great Hall chimed three. What! Only three in the afternoon! It seemed an age since Dalrymple had set out, and yet it was only four hours! What was she to do now? She thought of taking a turn round the park, but looking out of the window, she saw that the sky was darkening and threatening rain. Then she thought of the East Wing. It would be an interesting diversion to explore it, and surely no harm could come of it. She certainly had no thought of finding a bloodstained floor and the bodies of former wives hung on the wall, as in the Bluebeard tale, and she felt it equally unlikely that she would meet the ghost of Hell-Fire Dalrymple's murdered serving maid. Perhaps the worse she had to fear was the rotting floors – but even that, she realised, had been a mere excuse which her husband had made before he told her the truth. But what about the strict interdiction he had made before his departure? She considered this seriously for a moment. Of course he did not want her to see the private apartments of his former wife. He had realised that it might upset her – and she admitted to herself that that was the real danger. Well, perhaps she had better not go after all.

So after a few minutes more spent in reflections of a similar kind, Augusta decided that the best way to fill up her time would be to write a letter to her sister, so she made her way up the stairs and into her bedroom where she sat down at her writing desk. She pulled open the drawer to find writing materials, and the first thing she saw was – the keys, lying just where she had put them. The temptation was too much. She swept up the keys, and without pausing to consider what she was doing, went straight to the East Wing and unlocked the door.

It creaked on its hinges as she pushed it open, and a stale smell enveloped her. Augusta found herself in a series of apartments not unlike those of the West Wing, but with everything covered in dust sheets, and dust and cobwebs everywhere. It was gloomy as the windows were shuttered, but enough light penetrated through the gaps to enable her to see – and what she saw was very commonplace – no blood on the floor, no maid servant's ghost! Nor was there anything to indicate the presence of Dalrymple's first wife. Augusta felt herself relax, and she continued on until she reached the door leading to the tower, which she found to be locked. However, she tried the same key again, and it worked. The door led on to a large room at the bottom of the tower which had once been used as a drawing room. However, it was almost too dark to see in there, as heavy velvet curtains had been drawn across the shuttered windows. Augusta went to the nearest window, swept back the curtains, and folded back the shutter, and a weak January afternoon light revealed the contents of the room.

There was something different about this apartment that filled Augusta with curiosity – but what was it? She looked around for a while and then realised what it was. There were no dust sheets – and no dust. The room had the air of being used quite recently, which seemed strange after the series of long disused apartments. Then she caught sight of a portrait hanging over the mantlepiece. It was a portrait of a beautiful young woman. Augusta's heart missed a beat. "It is she!" she said aloud.

She went over for a closer look and saw a sad, pale face of a woman of about eighteen years of age. It was a beautiful face. More beautiful than I am, reflected Augusta with a pang of jealousy, but another voice in her head added, but less animated. She looks like a spiritless, passive little thing – not at all a suitable wife for one so strong as Fitzwilliam. It was thus that she consoled herself.

Augusta realised that she was straining to see, and a clap of thunder from outside told her the cause. The storm had come on, and the dark clouds were obscuring what little there was left of the day.

I must hurry, she thought, as she made her way upstairs to take a quick look at the upper apartments.

The staircase gave on to a small landing and a door which led to the principal bedroom. The room was completely dark, so as before, Augusta felt her way to the nearest window, drew the curtains and opened the shutters. A dull light picked out the outlines of the room. There was the bed, and there was the dressing table. At the far end of the room was a fireplace with a full-length portrait of Celia Dalrymple hanging over it, and to one side, another portrait showing Celia and Fitzwilliam together – that cost poor Augusta another pang of jealousy! In the centre of the room was a small table where she noticed books and implements for drawing had been left. Once again, it seemed that the room had seen recent use.

She was puzzling over this when a sudden flash of lightening filled the room with a livid radiance, and for a split second, Augusta thought she saw the ghost of Celia Dalrymple. She had certainly seen something – a full length sad-faced figure in a white robe standing at the other end of the room! Her blood ran cold, and she was desperate for more light. She pulled the dust sheet from the dressing table and scrabbled around in the drawers hoping to find a candle – but there was only a tinder box. A terrific crash of thunder made her jump, and the tinderbox fell to the ground, falling open and scattering its contents. Frantically, she fell on her hands and knees and gathered them up again – not that they were much good without a candle. Then an idea came to her. She looked for the sconces along the wall, and though she could not see clearly, felt each one, looking for a candle end. At last she found one, struck a light from the tinder box, and breathed a sigh of relief as the light filled the room. It was only one small flame, but after that threatening darkness, it seemed like a veritable sun. She scanned the room nervously, then breathed an even bigger sigh of relief as she saw her 'ghost' – the full length portrait had been lit up in a preternatural way by the sudden flash of lightening. Just then, the lightening flashed again, repeating the effect – but this time, instead of recoiling with horror, she laughed at her previous gullibility. "That is what comes of reading gothic novels!" she said aloud.

It was time to go. The candle end was guttering and it was now quite dark outside. Augusta hurried down the stairs, and made her way quickly through the empty apartments, finally locking the main door behind her, and leaning on it with a sigh of relief.

CHAPTER 5

"I've been looking for you everywhere," said an unexpected voice.

Augusta nearly jumped out of her skin, but looking round, saw that it was only Mrs Dufton. Since it must be quite obvious where she had been, Augusta felt that the best policy would be to brazen it out. After all, Mrs Dufton had no way of knowing that her husband had forbidden her to enter it.

"I've been exploring the East Wing," she said coolly.

"Rather you than me!" said Mrs Dufton, "especially on a night like this!"

Augusta was curious. "Why so?" she enquired.

"Well, it was there that the former Mrs Dalrymple lay in her sickness, and it was there that she died, and so everybody believes 'tis haunted by her ghost."

A thrill of horror ran down Augusta's spine as she realised that she had repeated almost word for word what Bertha had said to Matilda in *Wolfenbach* – but of course, it was merely a coincidence; or a better explanation might be – a commonplace superstition.

"Why should they believe that?" said Augusta. "Must every death result in a haunting?"

"Well, ma'am, it was the manner of her death that got folks talking. You see, she came here as a young healthy girl, and within a year she was dead – and there were strange circumstances surrounding it. Madam's maidservant, Betty, and Amelia, that was her companion, both disappeared at the same time. The master said that Amelia had gone home to Exeter, but no-one saw her go, and no-one ever heard of her again. He said that, of course, with madam dead, her maidservant was no longer needed, and had been sent away. But it was the same story – no-one saw her go, and no-one ever heard of her again."

"What did she die of?"

"Consumption, they say, but I have seen consumption before, and it is a long lingering death. It is true she was very bad, coughing blood and all – but suddenly she was gone – too suddenly for my liking."

"So what do you think happened?"

"Well, ma'am, it is not for me to say," said Mrs Dufton, becoming defensive, "I am only telling you the gossip from below stairs. These stories have a way of getting out of hand, as you know. Belike nothing untoward happened."

Augusta caught at these words. "So there are some who think that something untoward did happen?"

"Lord, ma'am! If I were to tell you what folk say I should lose my place! My lips are sealed from now on! It is an out and out colander to say that he made away with her."

"You mean 'calumny', I think," said Augusta, but as she observed that Mrs Dufton was becoming distressed, resolved not to press her further, and changed the subject.

"What were you wanting when you were looking for me?"

Mrs Dufton looked much relieved to be back on safe territory. "Why, I only wanted to know what you wanted for dinner, but as I could not find you, it will have to be mutton."

"That is perfectly satisfactory," said Augusta, and with

that Mrs Dufton went away to tell the cook, breathing an audible sigh of relief as she did so. Augusta went to the Withdrawing Room again, but seeing *Wolfenbach* lying open at the place where she had left off, she turned round in disgust, and decided to go up and change for dinner.

As Augusta sat in solitary state at the 40-place table, Her mind was racing over the events of the day, and the tangled tale told by Mrs Dufton. Of course, she did not for a minute believe that her dear Fitzwilliam could be guilty of so foul a deed, but there was certainly some mystery surrounding the death of his former wife, and she felt that it would be for the good of all if she could get to the bottom of it – most importantly, it would put an end to those unpleasant rumours. So she decided that she would visit the East Wing again – of course, when it was broad daylight! She was a practical, sensible person, and did not believe in the existence of ghosts, but she was all too aware what a dark night coupled with a vivid imagination could do!

Later that night, as she was preparing for bed, she went to the window and pulled back the curtain. The storm had died down, and the landscape was still. She could see, to the extreme left, the curve of the East Wing, and the dark shape of the East Tower. It was a sad contrast to the West Wing, in which, despite the present low occupancy of the building, lights could be seen in some of the windows. Then she saw – or thought she saw – a brief flicker of light in the topmost window of the East Tower. But it could not be! Surely it was her imagination! No. There it was again! She watched for a little longer to make sure, but the light did not reappear. After a while, she decided to attribute it to an overworked imagination, drew the curtain, and got into bed.

CHAPTER 6

Augusta whiled away the morning thinking over the events of the previous evening, and wondering if she could pluck up the courage to enter the East Wing again. It was raining outside, so she had nothing better to do than tour the apartments, particularly the Picture Gallery and the Library. In the Library, she was drawn to the shelf of gothic novels, and her eyes fell once again on *The Castle of Wolfenbach*, which the maid had picked up from the Withdrawing Room and returned to its proper place. She took it down again, found her place, and continued reading. After several pages she to the scene in which Matilda decides to spend a night in the haunted part of the castle. This is what she read:

Turning her eyes to the window, she saw a light glide by from the opposite wing, which her rooms fronted, and which Bertha had informed her was particularly haunted. At first she thought it was imagination; she arose and placed her candle in the chimney; and seated herself at the window, and very soon after she saw a faint glimmering light pass a second time; exceedingly surprised, but not terrified, she continued in her situation: she saw nothing further. She at length determined to go to rest, but with an intention to visit every part of the house the following day.

She was struck with the similarity with what had happened the night before when, she too, had seen a light in the opposite wing; and also by Matilda's courage in determining to explore. She felt that she could do no less, and laying down the book, went back to her bedroom to retrieve her keys, and from thence to the East Wing.

As it was early afternoon, she had no fear of being deprived of light, but she took a candle with her just in case. The apartments were filled with gloom, though the light penetrating through the cracks in the shutters was more than enough to see. The lower apartment of the tower was quite dark because, as before, heavy curtains had been drawn across the windows. She walked to the nearest window, drew back the curtain, opened the shutter, and the reassuring light of day flooded into the room – but as it did so, she was filled with thrill of horror. This was the same window that she had unshuttered the day before – so who had closed the shutter and drawn the curtain? Mrs Dufton? Possibly, but she recalled Dalrymple telling her that she did not have a key to these apartments. If not Mrs Dufton, who then? A quick look around the room showed that nothing else had changed, so feeling somewhat reassured, she climbed the stairs to the first floor. Once again, the room was in darkness. Once again, she opened the shutters of the same window – and once again she turned and saw the figure.

She cried out in surprise, and reeled with the shock to the extent that a momentary blackness overcame her. She staggered, slumped in the nearest chair, took several deep breaths, rubbed her eyes and looked again.

The figure was still there, exactly as she had seen it the night before – the sad-faced Celia in the long white gown. Nor was it the portrait, which hung on the wall close behind her. Whoever, or whatever it was, was real – a real person, or a real – ghost! (can there be such a thing as a real ghost? – or is that what scholars would call an oxymoron?)

But then Augusta got a grip of herself. She was in Clyfton, after all, not the Castle of Wolfenbach, and in England, not some half-civilised region of Romania, and the nineteenth century, not the Middle Ages!

"Who are you?" said Augusta trying to control her shaking voice.

"More to the point, who are you?" replied the figure.

"I am mistress of this house," said Augusta, not so much in pride, as to assert her right to be here, and to question this person.

The figure responded with a faint laugh as though she thought the idea of Augusta as mistress of the house was ridiculous. "It is I who am mistress of this house," she replied, "or should be."

Augusta, feeling certain now that this was no spectre, but a creature of flesh-and-blood like herself, responded, "What on earth do you mean by that?"

The figure sighed, and indicated the portrait on the wall. Then pointed the other portrait, the one showing Celia and Dalrymple together.

"So you are Celia?" said Augusta, filled now with a new horror.

"And as such, mistress of Clyfton," she said, "so I say again, who are you, and what are you doing here?"

Augusta replied, though with none of her former confidence. "I am Mrs Dalrymple."

Celia replied, "You cannot be Mrs Dalrymple while I live!"

Augusta slumped back into the chair again, overcome by a torrent of confusing emotions. Seeing this, Celia sat down beside her, and spoke in more soothing tones.

"I see you are much distressed – so should I be in your place, but if you will hear me out, I will give you a full explanation. Then it is up to you to decide how you will act."

Augusta nodded weakly.

"I was married to Mr Dalrymple six years ago this May. Our first year was one of untold bliss – but oh! he tired of me. He contrived to find an excuse for setting me aside, and he declared I was mad. He even went so far as to bribe Dr Mason to certify me as such. But as you can see – I am quite sane. I am not raving, am I? I am well-groomed and well-dressed, and my words are rational – if unwelcome."

Augusta said, "You seem perfectly sane to me – though I confess I have never met a madman so I have no standard of comparison."

"He said we should sleep in separate apartments, and began to sleep in the main house – for I have always preferred this dear little tower. Then one day I awoke to find myself a prisoner. Yes, it true! Look!"

She went to the unshuttered window and tried to raise the sash, but it would not move. "See!" she said, "locked! And every other window in this tower, and the door down below — locked!"

Just then another woman entered the room, "Excuse me, madam," she said, "but you must not talk to strangers."

"Do not tell me what to do!" snapped Celia. Then turning to Augusta again, she said, "At least Mr Dalrymple left me the support of my companion."

"You must come away, ma'am," said the companion again, and with that she took her by the hand and led her to the staircase.

"Wait!" called Augusta, "I need to ask you some more questions."

She hurried down the stairs after them, but when she entered the room below, they were nowhere to be seen. She went to the next door, and looked into the next apartment, but they were not there, either. How strange! They seemed to have disappeared into thin air! Perhaps they were ghosts, after all! Augusta shuddered at the thought, but had no stomach for any more, so made her way as quickly as she could back to the main house.

CHAPTER 7

Augusta ran up to her bedroom and lay there for a long time, tossing and turning, sometimes in a hot sweat, sometimes in a cold chill. Her mind raced over what she had seen and heard and turned it this way and that trying to make sense of it. In the bright light of day, flooding the room from the three tall windows, a supernatural explanation seemed the least likely — which was almost a pity, because the alternative explanation was even more unpalatable. Nevertheless, she had to force herself to accept that her beloved husband had at some point, and for some reason, tired of his first wife, and decided to confine her to the East Wing. He had staged some kind of fake death and funeral, no doubt by bribing the appropriate authorities, and had thus rid himself to all intents and purposes of his first wife. No wonder he had been so reluctant to tell her about his first marriage!

She sat up with sudden determination. She must write for help, and pray that help arrived before Dalrymple returned. She would write to her father and ask him to come at once with Mr Forester and a representative of the law. Accordingly, she went to the writing desk, penned an urgent missive, and commanded Betty to post it forthwith.

That task being accomplished, she paced up and down the room wondering what she should do next. One thing she was certain of – she would never again venture into the East Wing!

That night, she could not resist peering out to the East Tower. She watched it for some time, but there was no reappearance of the light in the upper window. She could only conclude that the mysterious inhabitants had taken greater care to ensure that their windows were shuttered and curtained.

On the following day, the hours seemed to drag. She kept going to her bedroom window which offered the best prospect of the drive as it wound down to the stream, over the bridge, and along the opposite side of the valley, but she had no real expectation of seeing her father's carriage. She calculated that he could not possibly have received the letter until this afternoon, at the earliest, and more likely not until the following morning. The journey would then take him half a day. Dalrymple was not expected until the following evening, so there was every chance that help would arrive in time.

Comforted by this thought, she whiled away the time in her usual way; wandering from apartment to apartment, and lingering most in the Picture Gallery and the Library. Once in the Library, it was inevitable that she would take down *The Castle of Wolfenbach*, even though she told herself that it was all nonsense, and was partly responsible for the trouble she now found herself in. Indeed, had she not been of such a sensible and strong-minded disposition, she might well have died with the shock of seeing Celia's 'ghost' on that first visit. Notwithstanding, she took the novel down to the Withdrawing Room, flicked through the pages, and finally settled down to read the following passage in which Matilda explores the most haunted part of the castle:

> *The instant she opened the door, another at the other end of the room was shut with great violence. The lady for a moment stood suspended; she trembled, and deliberated whether she should return or not; but recovering resolution, she entered; a candle was burning on a table, the windows were closed up, there were books and implements for drawing on the table; this convinced her the inhabitants were alive.*

Once again, Augusta was struck by the similarity of the narrative to her own experience. It occurred to her then that if she read on she might well find out how her adventure would end! – (Dear Reader! How often we identify the characters and circumstances in books with our own lives! But, of course, there can be no real connection. The author who wrote the story knew nothing of us and our concerns, and any connections are purely the result of our own fantasy.) Just then, Augusta heard the noise of an arrival in the Great Hall, and flung the book aside for the last time. It is just as well that she did, for had she read of the fate of Matilda, and linked it to her own, she would have only added to her distress!

She hurried down the great staircase and saw before her, her father, Mr Forester and some other unknown gentleman. It was a miracle that they should be there so soon – though perhaps not such a miracle in these days of Post-Chaises which travel along smooth turnpike roads at 16 mph! She ran to her father and threw himself into his arms.

"There, there," he said complacently. "What ever the trouble is, I'm sure these gentlemen will sort it out."

He then introduced Mr Wilson, a Justice of the Peace, who was accompanied by two officers of the law. "We did not delay. We came straight up the Great North Road, and called at Derby for these gentleman. Now, if you could tell us about your trouble."

Augusta's heart missed at beat. It was one thing to stand in front of Celia in the North Tower and listen to her sorry tale – but to make these gentleman believe it – quite another.

She showed them into the Withdrawing Room and called for some light refreshment, then she tried to tell her story.

"Mr Dalrymple has been married before," she began.

Mr Harlow raised an eyebrow. "It is the first I heard of it. He should have told us before – but it is hardly a capital offence."

"Well, the long and short of it is that his first wife did not die, as he told me – she is here – imprisoned in the East Wing."

Mr Harlow and Mr Forester received this information with very different reactions. Mr Forester seemed to boil with rage which expressed itself in the deep red flush that came into his face, Mr Harlow's face, on the other hand, betrayed a slight smile which seemed to suggest that he thought that imprisoning one's wife in the attic was not such a bad idea, especially in the case of a wife like his own. Mr Wilson's reaction was of a more practical nature: "It is a strange tale, but we can soon get to the bottom of it if we go into the East Wing and talk to the lady."

Just then another arrival was heard, and it was only a

matter of minutes before Dalrymple walked into the room.

"I was able to get away early," he said to Augusta. "But I see we have guests. Your father and uncle I know..." he made a slight bow as he said these words, "...but I have not the pleasure of an acquaintance these other gentleman."

Mr Harlow introduced them briefly, and Dalrymple's brow darkened. "And what business, pray, brings Officers of the Law to Clyfton?"

At this, Mr Forester, who could control himself no longer, stood up and barked the accusation. "You, sir! You are a bigamist!"

Dalrymple looked surprised, but seemed in perfect control of himself. "I have been called many things in my life, sir, but never that!" he retorted.

Then he looked at Augusta. "My dear, can you explain what all this is about?"

Augusta could hardly bring herself to say the words 'East Wing', but she did and blushed to the roots of her hair. Dalrymple shook his head sadly. She knew what he was thinking, and admired the self-control with which he held back the accusations which he must have longed to throw at her.

Mr Wilson took over, and made the accusation in a more measured way, as befits a representative of the law, "In short, sir, you are accused of unlawfully imprisoning your wife in the East Wing, and illegally marrying Miss Harlow."

Dalrymple was scornful, "And what evidence do you have to support such a tall tale?"

"What evidence do you have to deny it?" interposed Mr Forester.

Mr Dalrymple turned to Mr Wilson and said, not without irony, "I believe, sir, that it is still the case in England that a man is innocent until proved guilty?"

(Dear Reader! Would that were still the case today, but sadly, this Ancient Right of every Briton is being relentless undermined, not least by the pernicious DBS).

Mr Wilson said, "Indeed, sir, that is the case," and looked reprovingly at Mr Forester in the hope of preventing further interference. "What I suggest, therefore," he continued, "is that we find the lady in question, and ask her to tell us her story."

"You may do as you please, sir, if it will bring an end to this – farce," said Dalrymple. "I believe my wife has the one and only key to the East Wing. Would you be so good as to give it to him, Augusta?"

Mr Wilson asked her to show him the way, but she replied that she had vowed never to go in the East Wing again, and gave him instead minute directions as to the tower and the upper chamber where she had last seen the woman. Mr Harlow and Mr Forester stayed behind, thinking to protect Augusta against a possible outburst of rage from Dalrymple, but he simply sat down in an easy chair and hid himself behind a newspaper.

It was a long time before the others reappeared, but at last they did so. Augusta could see straight away from Mr Wilson's apologetic air that their search had been unavailing.

"I am very sorry to have troubled you, sir," he said to Mr Dalrymple, "but there is no sign of anyone in any of the apartments, dressing rooms, or closets."

Dalrymple nodded indifferently, as though he expected no other outcome, but Mr Forester was on his feet at once, "Sir, I protest! My niece has been greatly wronged! Surely you do not intend to leave it at that? You should search the whole house – the woman must be found!"

"There is an easier way than that," said Dalrymple, with a warning note of irony in his voice which, however, Mr Forester did not notice.

They all looked at him to hear what it was.

"You want to see my first wife? Very well, go to Tickhill churchyard, and dig her up!"

Dalrymple's words, shocking as they were, had been well chosen. They all realised that that would put an end to the matter once and for all – but who could sanction such a macabre process on the basis of a mere accusation? Mr Wilson spoke for them all, "That will not be necessary. Of course, if I had strong grounds to suspect foul play, I have the authority order an exhumation, but I believe there may be a simpler explanation, which may be something along the lines of a young woman, left alone in a huge mansion on a stormy night and..." here his eyes turned to the discarded novel, and the others followed his glance, "...reading such stuff as that!"

Dalrymple, seeming satisfied, stood up. "Thank you Mr Wilson. I own that I share a part of the blame for leaving – my wife – here, alone, so soon after our marriage."

Mr Wilson nodded, and soon after, he took his leave, taking his officers with him. As soon as they had gone, Dalrymple turned to his guests and said, "Well, I hope you are satisfied. I think Mr Wilson's explanation was a probable one, and that this..." here he took up *Wolfenbach*, "...is at least partly responsible. I am well-known as a lover of books, but on this occasion..." he completed his sentence by throwing the book onto the fire.

Mr Harlow watched it burn with an amused twinkle in his eye. Mr Forester was mollified to some extent, but still looked uncertain. Augusta felt deeply embarrassed and wished she had thrown the book on the fire herself before she had ever begun it.

"I hope you will join us for dinner," said Dalrymple after the temporary flare caused by the book had died down, "and perhaps you would also honour us with an overnight stay. I'm sure my wife will appreciate the opportunity of hearing the Tickhill news and enjoying the society of her father and uncle. Now, if you will excuse me, I have some business papers to attend to."

With that, he left the room to arrange his papers, and

then to dress for dinner.

"So, gothic novels, was it?" said Mr Harlow, quite enjoying the ridiculousness of the situation.

"She was really there!" protested Augusta. "I know the difference between reality and imagination!"

"After a stormy night and a dose of *Wolfenbach*?" said Mr Harlow smiling.

"I believe you," said Mr Forester, comfortingly. "But if she really was there, why couldn't Mr Wilson find her?"

"Because she disappears!" cried Augusta, and went on to relate how she had followed her downstairs and then found no sign of her, though she searched everywhere.

Mr Harlow laughed. Mr Forester looked uncomfortable.

"Oh, I am not saying she disappeared into thin air, but perhaps she went through a secret door!"

Mr Harlow's laugh got louder. "Oh this is good! It is secret doors now!"

"Father!" she reprimanded him. "This is serious! It might be me next! What shall I do?"

But her father could not be prevailed upon to take the matter seriously. Instead, it was Mr Forester who replied: "Perhaps there is some mystery, but one which is not as bad as your imagination paints. After all, I recall you telling us that Mr Dalrymple did not at first tell you that he had been married before."

Augusta replied in the affirmative.

"Then perhaps he has not, even yet, told you the whole truth."

"But what could it be?"

Mr Forester shook his head. "How am I to know? Perhaps some servants playing a prank. But seriously, you should speak to your husband and give him a chance to tell you the whole, unvarnished truth."

This suggestion made such eminent sense that Augusta resolved to act upon it.

CHAPTER 8

It was Dalrymple, however, who raised the subject first. As they were undressing for bed, he said, "Augusta, you broke my trust. I specifically forbade you to go into the East Wing, and as a result of your disobedience, we had to suffer that embarrassing scene with Mr Wilson – though I pride myself that I carried it off rather well under the circumstances."

Augusta, however, was prepared. "If you had told me the whole truth in the first place, I would not have been a victim to curiosity."

Dalrymple thought about this for a moment. "I own it, and I also realise that I owe you a full explanation. Sit down, my love, and listen carefully, and I will unfold the whole sorry tale."

Augusta sat down at her dressing table, her heart beating in anticipation of the terrible things she was a bout to hear.

"I think I told you that my former wife, Celia, died of consumption. Well, that is not strictly true..."

Augusta's heart missed a beat.

"She was murdered..."

Augusta cried out in horror.

"No, no," responded Dalrymple. "You misunderstand! She was not murdered by me, but by her female companion."

Augusta relaxed a little.

"I think I told you that Celia's female companion was Amelia, her sister. Well, she loved her very much and could not bear to see her suffering – for everyday she coughed up her lungs, choked on the mucus – how she suffered! But you know the disease, I think. I will not elaborate on it. It is too painful. The worse thing of all for those who loved her, was the knowledge that no cure was possible. She would linger like this, perhaps for months, in excruciating agony, and then would die in the end. Well, her sister – acting out of love – mixed arsenic with her usual dose of laudanum, and put her out of her misery. An act of generosity and love – one which I would call, applying the Greek I learned at Cambridge – *euthanasia* – but which the authorities would describe with a harsher word – murder! It was impossible to hide the distinctive smell of kernels, and the doctor noticed it straight away. Fortunately, I was in London on the day she died, so there was no danger of me being implicated – and Amelia was soon suspected. Ah! what a dilemma I was in! I knew she had acted out of love, and could not bear to see her hang, and so I made a plan. I told the authorities that she had fled, and the maid with her, and hid them in the basement of the East Wing. There are extensive apartments down there – as there are under the whole house – and I made them very comfortable. So for the last five years, Amelia and Sally have been living there..."

"But this is just another fabrication! I saw Celia with my own eyes!" protested Augusta.

Dalrymple smiled sadly. "No, you did not see Celia. How could you? She is long dead. The woman you saw was her sister – and very like they are too."

"I'm sorry," said Augusta, "go on."

"Well, that brings me to my present problem, and I have to be honest and say that I have no idea what to do about it. Perhaps you will have a suggestion."

"Go on," Augusta encouraged him.

"For a few years the arrangement was satisfactory. Amelia had Sally to look after her. I visited her sometimes, and she wanted for no material comfort, but...but it is far from being a normal way of life, and I began to suspect it was taking a toll on her mind."

"You mean...?"

"Yes, she started to go mad. She spent more and more time in the East Tower, though I told her it was dangerous to do so. The servants would occasionally hear a noise, or see a light, and that's when the rumours began. Latterly, I believe that she thinks that she is Celia, and she acts out the scenes she must have observed as Celia's companion – Celia brushing her hair in the mirror, Celia wearing on her large and varied wardrobe, Celia sleeping in her bed, and so on. So what am I to do with her?"

"You could hand her over to the authorities," suggested Augusta, "surely she will not hang if she is mad?"

Dalrymple thought about it. "It is a possibility, but if they do not hang her, they will confine her to some abysmal mental hospital – Bethlehem Hospital, for example, or Bedlam, as I hear they call it now."

Augusta shuddered.

"So what will you do?"

"I could try to carry on as before, but there is an increasing chance she will be discovered. Perhaps I should recruit more helpers, as she is getting beyond the power of Sally to control."

Augusta sighed. "At least it is our shared problem now, and not something that comes between us?"

"And did you really think that I was a bigamist?" said Dalrymple with a wry smile.

"I didn't know what to think," said Augusta. "Everything seemed so topsy-turvey..." she laughed. "...but that is too childish a word to describe how it feels when your whole world is falling apart."

Dalrymple took her in his arms. "My dearest, loveliest Augusta. I am so sorry. It is all my fault. I should have told you everything before we married – but oh! I feared it would frighten you off. Such a strange tale – a dead wife, a closed up wing, a murderess in the basement!"

"It would make a good novel," said Augusta, "better than any of those in the library! Why I might even..."

"Don't you ever think of it. You must leave that to the likes of Mrs Radcliffe!"

"Perhaps. But what are we to do about Amelia?"

"I don't know," said Dalrymple solemnly. "I'm sure

we'll think of something. In the meantime, I will get more help for Sally."

CHAPTER 9

Life at Clyfton soon settled into such a pleasant routine that the East Wing was almost forgotten. However, about two weeks after the incidents described above, Dalrymple received a letter, and after reading it, announced to Augusta.

"It seems the business of Buxton Woods is complete, so I'm afraid I have to go to London to complete the transaction. I will stay as before with Colonel Shelby and my sister, but I promise to be back within the week."

"Must you go?" said Augusta.

"I afraid I must. I have the woods at a good price, and must seal the transaction. But you will be perfectly comfortable here, that is to say, as long as you don't go poking about in the East Wing!"

"Have no fear!" said Augusta, "a thousand horses couldn't drag me in there again!"

"Nevertheless, here are the keys should any emergency arise with regard to Amelia. But Sally has help now, so I am confident you will have no problems in that direction."

When Dalrymple had gone, Augusta entertained herself in the usual way, but, the afternoon being fine, though with a chilling Easterly wind, she preferred to spend it in the Walled Garden which afforded the opportunity to be outside with the benefit of some shelter from the high wall. On the whole, she felt that a breath of bracing January air would be much better for her than moping around in the Picture Gallery or Library. She even took a turn around the park, and visited the Folly, though without bringing *Udolpho*, as she had quite lost her taste for gothic novels. Accordingly, when stepped into bed, she found that a healthy tiredness overwhelmed her quickly, and soon she was in the depths and a profound and healthful slumber.

She awoke suddenly in time to hear the Laughton grandfather clock chime twelve, and assumed that she had been woken up by the triple chimes that preceded the tolling of the hour. The room was quite dark. The fire had burnt out, and even the embers had lost their redness. The curtains were drawn, though the shutters were still open, allowing the faintest of illumination to alleviate the darkness.

Augusta tossed and turned. Something was making her uneasy, and she became convinced that she was not alone in the room. She reached for the tinderbox beside her bed and tried to strike a light so that she could light the candle, but her fumbling hands dropped the flint, and it rolled somewhere under the bed. She was becoming agitated now, and rolling quickly out of bed, ran to the centre window and flung back the curtain. The light of a full moon streamed into the room illuminating everything with a ghostly light – and there stood, shining like a ghost in her white dress – the figure of Celia Dalrymple.

Augusta gasped, and it was only with an effort of self-discipline that she forced herself to remember that this was not a ghost, but a human being (albeit a mad one) and was not Celia Dalrymple, but her sister, Amelia.

"What are you doing here?" she said, as soon as she could command her voice.

"There is no need to be afraid," answered Amelia. "I know he told you that I was mad..."

How could she know that? wondered Augusta.

"...but I am as sane as you are, and to answer your question, I am come here to warn you."

"Warn me?"

"Yes. Do not forget that there is another wing to this house, and when my beloved husband feels the urge to take a third wife. That is where you will find yourself – locked in!"

"It is no use," said Augusta as calmly as she could. "I

know the truth!"

Amelia laughed with a dry cackle which chilled Augusta to the bone with its suggestion of madness, and its hint that she knew better.

"I know what he told you..." she said.

How could she? thought Augusta.

"...but that man is a consummate liar. He always tells a part-truth. You had a little of it when he confessed to being married, and now you have a little more – but how do you know he has told you the whole truth?"

"And what is the whole truth?" said Augusta in the same tone that Pontius Pilate might have used, viz., with a note of scepticism.

"It is a pity that you could not persuade the Justice to exhume Celia's coffin! Oh! you would have found a body, all right! The body of my dear sister, Amelia. He said I was mad and tried to lock me away in the tower, and she tried to stop him – with the inevitable result!"

"Then you are Celia?" said Augusta.

"Have you not seen my likeness many times?"

"Dalrymple said that you and your sister were very much alike."

"Ah! he is a clever one with words, that man! We are alike, yes, but we are not twins. It is – or I should say 'was' – not difficult to distinguish between us."

Augusta thought for a moment. By now the numinous horror of the moonlight-filled room, and the ghostly-looking figure was somewhat alleviated, and Augusta knew how she might alleviate it further.

"Excuse me a moment," she said, then kneeling down, felt under the bed, retrieved the flint, struck it against the steel with a surer hand, and within a matter of seconds her candle spread its warm, human light around the room. The ghostly figure took on a little colour which showed the all-too human blemishes of her skin, and the cream colour of her robe. Augusta felt her courage revive at the sight.

"You said you came here to warn me. What did you want to warn me about?"

Celia, or Amelia, cackled again, and replied, "Only this: that you must leave my husband, or I will be revenged on you all!"

She took a few steps back into the gloom, and by the time Augusta had picked up her candle to see better, she was gone. Augusta's blood ran cold – though not because of her sudden disappearance, for she guessed that she had probably mastered every secret panel and passageway in the whole rambling edifice. The worrying thing was that she could use that knowledge to steal in upon her at any time and plunge a knife into her bosom.

Augusta immediately ran downstairs, woke her maid, and wrote a letter to her husband. In it she said that Amelia was 'on the loose' and that for her own safety she was going to Oldcotes as soon as it was light, and would he please meet her there on his way back from London?

CHAPTER 10

They discussed the matter on the way back from Oldcotes, and decided that the time had come to put the matter in the hands of the authorities, which they would do the very next day. When Augusta expressed her fear of spending even one more night at Clyfton with that woman 'on the loose', Dalrymple laughed her fears away.

"Do not worry," he said confidently. "I am a light sleeper, and I will have loaded pistols beside the bed, though to be frank, I doubt very much whether she would stoop to an act of violence, deranged though she is."

After a late dinner, they went to bed early, fully resolved to rise with the dawn and be rid of the matter once and for all. Augusta found it hard to sleep at first, but after her long journey, and with the strong body of her husband beside her, her fears soon subsided and she fell asleep.

She was jerked awake by a terrific crash that sounded like all the thunderstorms she had ever heard rolled into one. A moment later, she heard her husband's voice exclaim: "Dammit! Missed!" then another voice, "Sir, sir! Do not kill me for the love of God! It is only me, Sally!"

"The devil," cursed Dalrymple, rolling out of bed. "What do you mean creeping up on us in the darkness like that! You nearly got yourself killed!"

Sally seemed much distressed. "I'm sorry, master, but it is an emergency. I had no time to think of a candle; and in any case, I hardly need one – look!"

With that, she rushed to the window and threw back the curtains. A livid orange light filled the sky, and Augusta saw at once that the East Wing was engulfed in torrents of flame. When Dalrymple saw it, he growled, "Damn her, it is her revenge! But how can I blame her! She is quite mad and believes herself to be Celia. Quickly! We must raise the household!"

"Will you not try to save her?" said Augusta with a feeling of pity as she thought how horrible it would be to die in such a conflagration.

Dalrymple looked at her in surprise. "What! Risk my life for a madwoman. No. I will be frank with you. Far better for us all that she dies in the blaze. What is much more important is that we save Clyfton! We can do it, too, if we drench the nearer part of the East Wing, and take care to extinguish any burning matter that floats this way in the breeze."

So the great battle for Clyfton began. Dalrymple had Augusta taken to the gatekeeper's cottage, but himself stayed behind to direct the fire-fighting operations. Reinforcements were brought in from Tickhill, along with a horse-drawn pump which was used to pump water from the stream and into the East Wing.

By dawn, all that was left of the East Wing was a

blackened shell – but the main edifice was untouched.

"What happened to Celia – I mean, Amelia?" said Augusta.

"She was seen on the battlements at about 1 o'clock," said Dalrymple matter-of-factly, "but the roof fell in soon after, and she went down with it."

"It is a sad end for one who did no evil."

"Indeed," said Dalrymple, "so I will ensure that she has a worthy funeral, and that the record is put straight. All shall know how she helped her sister, and she will beyond the retributive malice of the law."

The funeral, and more particularly the obituary sermon, put an end to the damaging rumours that had been circulating amongst the staff and around the village. All agreed that it had been a tragic tale: the one sister dying of consumption, the other trying to spare her pain, and sacrificing her life in the process. Dalrymple was criticised in some quarters for trying to hush the matter up, but none doubted his good motives. For himself, the only two things Dalrymple regretted was the fact that he had not told Augusta everything before they were married, and that he had been betrayed into a most ungentlemanly outburst of profane language when he had almost shot Sally by mistake.

Life at Clyfton was almost back to normal, when one morning Dalrymple caught Augusta struggling downstairs with a huge pile of books. "Whatever are you doing with those," he said. "You must get used to asking the servants to do such things. Here, at Clyfton, there is only one job you have to do for yourself, and I needn't tell you what that is."

"This is something I particularly want to do for myself," returned Augusta.

"Why, what is it?"

"I am taking this pile of gothic novels outside and I am going to make a bonfire of them."

"Is that because they so misled you?"

"Not at all," laughed Augusta, "it is because they are so badly written that I think I can write a better one."

"And what will you call it?"

"Why, what else but – *Dalrymple's Dark Secret!*"

7. THE BAG MUCK STRIKE

The 'Bag Muck' Strike took place in Denaby Main and Cadeby Collieries in 1902-1903. Bag Muck was an uneven layer of rock that ran through the seam of Barnsley coal, measuring from 24 inches to 36 inches in thickness. When thin and soft, the colliers had no objection to digging it out, but when it was hard, it cost the miners time and effort to dispose of, time which a miner could spend digging out coal, and therefore earning money. My two grandfathers, Arthur Webster and William Roberts, lived through the events described in the following pages. They often talked about it, and I wish I had written down what they said.

I

It was Sunday afternoon, a time when the people of Conisbrough were generally relaxing. The men, having finished dinner, usually sat on low walls or other handy seats, and smoked and talked. But upon this special Sunday afternoon in late June no-one settled down to his ordinary pursuits, for the men stood talking in groups in the street, until, as the hour of four approached, there was a general move towards the Station Hotel. The Station Hotel was the meeting place of the Cadeby Lodge and convenient enough for the workmen of both pits who lived in Denaby Main or Conisbrough, though not for those men who lived in Mexborough. As there were too many men to be accommodated in the building, the meeting was held in the adjoining field.

Presently a group of some five or six men came up together, made their way through the throng, and took their stand on the edge of the tip, some twenty feet above the crowd. These were the delegates, the representatives of different branches of the Yorkshire Miners' Association.

Tom, after an inner struggle, had decided to forego the pleasure of seeing Gerty, and accompany his father and brother to the meeting. They were just in time to hear Mr Croft (the chairman of the Denaby Lodge) open the meeting. Croft had a reputation of being a fiery speaker. He would start quietly enough, then work himself up into red-faced frenzy. He started today in his quietest manner, as though determined to keep control of himself.

"It is hard lines when a matter of £3 12s is knocked off the wages of four men. The wages are low enough as it is!"

His tone became higher and sharper as he said the last words. One of the men shouted, "Be calm, Croft!"

"In regard to the 'bag dirt' question, I urge you all to be united; if the coal-owners have their millions, they have not the labour, and I hope you will be prepared if it comes to a fight!"

By the time he reached the word 'fight', he was at his fiery best, and some of the men repeated the phrase: "Be calm!"

That phrase was to become the catchphrase of the strike, and it helped many a man to control himself when his feelings were getting the better of him.

The next speaker was Mr Henry Humphries, one of the officials of the Cadeby Lodge.

"I have always contended that the miners have nothing to do with the 'bag dirt', neither in getting it down or removing it, because it is not on the price list. Some years ago, when the price list was formed, the 'bag dirt' was not so thick as it is now, neither was it so hard to get down. Let me remind you that the men in the drift district at Denaby pit are the worst affected, but each miner at the two pits should make the case his own. It is the principle of every Union man that what was one man's grievance should be every man's grievance."

There was universal assent to this statement, with cries of "aye!" and "that's true!"

Mr John Nolan, the Denaby delegate, was the next to speak.

"The company cannot accuse us of being over-hasty in this matter. It has been bothering us for two years. When we took the case to the County Court, the judge, although he gave the case to the colliery company on a point of law, said he believed that the time had come when something ought to be done about it by way of a fresh price list for this thick 'bag dirt'.

The Heads of Lodges having made their speeches, it was time for some of the lesser officials to speak. The first was Mr Brocklesby. Tom swelled with pride as he saw his father step up onto the stand. It was the first time he had seen him in his role as a leader of men, even though a very minor one. He spoke in his customary broad accent, though with fewer dialect expressions than he used in everyday conversation. His subject was the men's grievances about stoppages for petty matters such as dirty coal and lost lockers, and the unfairness of the ridiculously low pay for pit lads, urging that it be increased to 1/3 per day.

After the speeches, a ballot was taken. The papers were handed round, marked by the men, and then put in the box. Tom, as he was under eighteen, was not allowed to vote, but he was quite sure that if he had he would have voted to go on strike. He had seen the bag muck at first hand, and his own work had been harder because of it. It was manifestly unfair that the miners should not paid for something that was taking up an increasing amount of their time and effort.

There was a long period of restless waiting while the votes were counted, and then to breathless anticipation, the results were read out by Mr Croft:

In favour: 1,136,
Against: 907
Majority in favour: 229

There were groans of disappointment as men did the mental arithmetic. They had not achieved the two-thirds majority necessary for a strike. The result of the ballot, nevertheless showed that there was a general feeling of discontent, and the following motion was unanimously adopted:

"That this meeting is of the opinion that the time has now arrived when some steps should be taken with reference to the deduction from men's wages for 'bag dirt' and fines for different things at Denaby and Cadeby Collieries; seeing that we have tried all in our power to come to some amicable understanding and failed, the only thing that is left for us to do is to stop the wheels at both collieries."

There was a cry of "Be calm, Croft!" accompanied by shouts of, "aye!" and, "that'll show 'em!"

All things considered, the general mood was positive. The problem of the 'bag muck' had been looming over them for a long time, and it felt good to have taken decisive action at last. The privations were yet to come, though the older miners, who remembered the strike of 1885, did not need to use their imagination to know what suffering lay before them.

"That's it, lad, tha's a man o' leisure now," said Dick to Tom, as they walked back home.

"Not quite," said Tom. "I've still got my church job."

"An' a good thing, too," said Mr Brocklesby. "That 7/6 is like to come in handy!"

"I'm going to ask Mr Mews if he can find more work for me," said Tom, encouraged.

But Mr Mews shook his head sadly when Tom told him the news. "So, they're out, are they? There'll be hard times ahead."

Tom saw his opportunity.

"That's why I wanted to ask you if there's any extra work for me – playing the organ, I mean."

Mr Mews pondered the question, then said, "Not much. But there's sometimes a funeral in the week that I can't get to. That'll pay 10/-, but…"

"What?"

"Are you sure the sight of the coffin won't upset you?"

Tom shuddered at the thought.

"Is there nothing else?"

"I'll ask around," said Mr Mews, "but there's no time to stand here chattering. Give out the service music."

II

It seemed strange not to have to get up for work the next morning, but when he did get up and went out into the village, he found that there was almost a holiday atmosphere. The men were enjoying the unaccustomed leisure. An ad hoc football match was taking place on the recreation ground, and men sat on low walls, smoking and chatting, as they usually did on Saturday or Sunday. They still had money in their pockets for tobacco, and for a few pints in the evening, so they were happy enough.

Tom went to Night School on Tuesday with renewed enthusiasm. For the first time he felt he could give the lesson the concentration it deserved, as he would not be tired out from his long shift. It seemed that the others felt the same. Indeed, there were more men there than there had been for months, as some of the dropouts had returned in the hope of finding something to do.

"No!" said Mr Andrews when they proffered their shillings. "Now that there's a strike on, I couldn't, in all conscience, take them. Now what I suggest is, you put your shilling in that box over there, and we will use it to buy bread for the children when times get hard."

That act of generosity did more for Mr Andrew's cause of passing on the torch of learning than any other thing that he said or did. It made them men feel that he was interested in them for their own sake, and not for the sake of eking out his modest salary.

Davies put his hand up. "Since there's a strike on, perhaps you could teach us more about Marxism."

Mr Andrews scratched his bristly head as he considered the suggestion.

"I have already told you that I don't know much about it," he said at last.

"Then tell us what you know," said Tom.

"Aye," said others in support.

Mr Andrews looked at the door as though he feared a council official might walk through it at that very moment.

"I wouldn't want to be thought subversive," he said, flushing and looking uncomfortable. "Otherwise, the council might close us down."

"Go on, we won't tell anybody," said Davies.

Mr Andrews looked at his desk, moved a pen-holder from one side to the other, then seemed to come to a decision.

"Very well, I'll tell you what we'll do. We will discuss a saying by Marx, and a saying by Jesus every week. You've had no religious education as yet, so we will be killing the birds of politics and religion with one stone."

While the men were unraveling his curious metaphor, he picked up a Bible from a bookshelf and flicked through the pages. He found what he wanted, marked the page with a scrap of paper, then put the Bible down again.

"But we will begin with Marx. Tell me what you think of this saying of his: From each according to his ability, to each according to his needs."

"I know I need a lot more than I've got!" said Williams.

"And what does Mrs Woodyeare do all day? Nothing!" said Davies.

"Be fair, she's an elderly widow," said Tom.

"Well then, the likes of her. The great folk. Huntin' shootin' fishin' – that's great fun for them, but it's not giving owt to society."

"Anything," corrected Mr Andrews.

"What about Doctor Clark?" said Williams. "He gives his medical skill, and in return he has a nice house, servants, good food."

"Aye, that's about right," said Davies, "but what about us. We give hard graft and get nothin'. You know what it's like, never mind the strike. Payday on Saturday, get things out o' pawn. Fill your pouch with baccy, drink a pint or too. Have a bit o' meat with yer Sunday dinner, but by Wednesday, everythin's in pawn again. Worra life!"

"It's not as bad as that!" said Williams.

"No, not when you've got one or two sons working. But if there's only one wage, and not a hewer's, life is hard!"

The men looked at each other in puzzlement, as though not knowing what to make of it all. Then Tom asked, "Can you explain it, sir?"

Mr Andrews shook his head. "I can't explain how things came to be how they are, or why Earl Fitzwilliam has everything and does nothing, while you have nothing even though you work long hours, but I can try to explain what

Marx meant. In his ideal society, each person would be motivated to work for the good of society despite the absence of a social mechanism compelling them to work, because work would have become a pleasurable and creative activity. Marx intended the initial part of his slogan, 'from each according to his ability' to suggest not merely that each person should work as hard as they can, but that each person should best develop their particular talents and thus be able to enjoy their work."

"What about cutting coal?" said Williams. "There's no talent in that, and no pleasure, so in Marx's ideal society it would never get done."

"And we'd all freeze to death!" quipped Adrian.

Mr Andrews stroked his chin.

"That's a difficult point to answer, and to be honest, I don't know how Marx would have answered it. All I can say is that men have not always delved for coal and they seemed to get on well enough. Perhaps coal is necessary to power that great engine that Marx called Capitalism. Without it there would be no factories, or railways, or steamships – but men have lived for thousands of years without those things."

There was a short silence while the students tried to conceive of a world without coal. Then Mr Andrews moved the discussion on with a change of topic. "Before we lose that word 'talent' let's consider the Parable of the Talents in Matthew's gospel. You all know it, I think, but to just to make sure, I'll go over it again: The parable tells of a master who was leaving his house to travel, and, before leaving, entrusted his property to his servants. According to the abilities of each man, one servant received five talents, the second servant received two talents, and the third servant received one talent. The property entrusted to the three servants was worth 8 talents, where a talent was a significant amount of money. Upon returning home, after a long absence, the master asks his three servants for an accounting of the talents he entrusted to them. The first and the second servants explain that they each put their talents to work, and have doubled the value of the property with which they were entrusted and both of them were rewarded. You remember the words of gospel: 'Well done, good and faithful servant; thou hast been faithful over a few things, I will make thee ruler over many things: enter thou into the joy of thy lord.' The third servant, however, had merely hidden his talent, had buried it in the ground, and was punished by his master. Now, how can we compare that to what Marx said?"

"Use your talents," said Tom, feeling secretly proud that he was developing his musical talent.

"Yes, Tom, that's right. All of you here have talent of some kind – or you wouldn't be here. What I hope to do in these classes is to develop it, then perhaps you will be able to find work that is satisfying, and if you can't do it as a job, at least you can do it as a hobby. Like Tom, here, with his music."

Tom, hoping to take attention from himself, said, "Or like my dad. His hobby is carpentry. He'll work for hours in our shed on bits of furniture. You should see what a fine job he did of my old organ! He stripped it down, mended the bellows, took out each reed and cleaned it, and then repolished the case. It's as good as new now!"

"It's like Fred Mercer's pigeons," said Davies.

"Or my allotment," said Williams.

"That's it," said Mr Andrews. "That's just what Marx was talking about – work that you enjoy doing, and you can do more and more of that kind of work, and perhaps even get paid for it, if you take Our Lord's advice and develop your talents."

The time had passed quickly becuase they had all been so absorbed in the subject. It had been an impromptu lesson, but Mr Andrews felt that it was lessons like that that made his job worthwhile, rather than the endless grind of times tables and lists of dates that he had to teach throughout the day.

As Tom was leaving, Mr Andrews called him aside.

"You are doing so well in your general education, that I would like you to start in my advanced class. That's on Thursday's, and our focus is arithmetic and book-keeping. We are working towards the Cambridge examination in book-keeping. I wasn't going to ask you until next academic year, but you will have so much time on your hands, I thought you might as well use it to advantage. You needn't bother with the fee, as I will be saying the same thing about the box to my advanced class."

The first thought that came into Tom's head was, "at last!" – the second was, "oh no! It clashes with choir practice!"

The following week. Mr Andrews gave them another quotation from Marx to discuss:

"The proletarians have nothing to lose but their chains. They have a world to win. Workingmen of all countries, unite!"

"What are 'proletarians', sir," asked Tom.

"Workers," said Mr Andrews. "Like all of us."

"But we're not in chains," said Williams, "We're free Englishmen!"

"It's true that you're not a serf," said Mr Andrews.

"What's a serf?" asked Tom.

Mr Andrews explained, then added, "or a slave."

They all knew what slaves were.

"Theoretically, any of you can down tools, leave the colliery, leave Denaby and look for another job in another town. But would it work?"

"Only if it was a mining job," said Williams. "I can't do nothing else."

Mr Andrews looked hard at him. "But you can. That's why you're here."

"What do you mean?" said Williams.

"If you improve your education, as you are doing right now, you may, perhaps become an overlooker or a deputy."

"But what about all the others?" said Davies.

"That's just it. Marx believed that if working men united they could overthrow the system and bring about a society in which they had a greater share of things."

"Nah!" scoffed Williams. "We don't want no revolution here, like them Rusky's had!"

"But it's happening now in a small way. The men are uniting to bring about better conditions of service."

"Aye, that's right," said Davies.

"And, bit by bit, they can bring about social change without a revolution."

"But how," said the skeptical Williams. "It's like I said before. The bosses have all the capital."

"A contemporary of Marx, a man called Engels, said that there should be common ownership of the means of production."

"What, the miners own the mines!" said Williams, incredulous.

"Well, perhaps not the miners, but the government," suggested Mr Andrews.

Williams laughed out loud – a somewhat forced laugh, but he wanted to emphasise what he thought of such an impossible idea.

"Yes, it's hard to believe it could ever happen," said Mr Andrews, "and I doubt it will happen in our lifetimes, and that's why I come back to my point that, though we have very little real freedom, we must do the best we can with what we have. Let's see what the Bible has to say on that topic."

He picked up his Bible and turned to a place that he had marked with a piece of paper.

"This is from Galatians: Stand fast therefore in the liberty wherewith Christ hath made us free, and be not entangled again with the yoke of bondage."

He paused for a moment, looked at the class over his spectacles, then said, "What do you think St Paul is saying about freedom here?"

Tom was quick to answer. He had heard so much about the Bible in church, and even though he didn't usually listen, he seemed to have soaked it up unconsciously.

"He's talking about freedom from sin."

"How can that apply to us?" said Mr Andrews.

"There's plenty o' sin in Conisbrough," said Williams.

"And even more in Denaby," said Davies. "Drinkin' the wages, gambling, wife-beating – and that's just for starters!"

"A lot of it arises from poverty," said Mr Andrews, "but the sad thing is, it reinforces poverty."

"So what are we supposed to do about it?" said Williams.

Mr Andrews shook his head. "It's not for me to preach to you. There's plenty of parsons to do that. Perhaps I should never have introduced the topics. Marx and Christianity are both controversial in their way."

After the class Mr Andrews asked Tom why he was still coming to the general class instead of the advanced class, and Tom told him about his clash.

"Well, stay here for now, Tom. There's no hurry just yet, and I'm sure it will sort itself out eventually."

The following Tuesday, Mr Andrews, abruptly changed back to Geography.

"This week we are going to start a Geographical case study which I hope you will find interesting – the Quest for the Source of the Nile."

"But what about..." Williams began.

Davies elbowed him and gave him a hard look. Word had got round that Mr Andrews had been 'nobbled' by the headmaster, and been warned off the teaching of controversial topics. But they had had their introduction to Marx, and if they wanted to know more it was up to them.

III

The mood on the streets of Conisbrough was now very different. After the initial bravado and anticipation of early victory, the money began to run out and stern reality set in. The mood was particularly bad in Denaby where the mine was almost the only employer. Conisbrough fared rather better due its wider range of employment. There was Kilner's Glassworks, Ashfield Brickyard, the Sickle Works, and the Eltsac Toffee Works, not to mention many smaller concerns, but compared to the vast number of men employed by the colliery company (over 3000 in the combined collieries), the number of their employees was a small proportion of the working population of the town.

Tom's family was a good example. Though three miners' wages were lost, Alice gave her mother all she earned as a maid at Old Hall – a paltry 5/- a week, but better than nothing, and Tom, of course, contributed his 7/6. There was also strike pay from the Union. The rates were: 9/- for a miner, 9/- for his eldest son, 4/6 for a second son and 1/- for every child. Thus the Brocklesby family income fell from around £5 2s 6d to £1 3s 6d.

They pawned what they could. The beautiful mahogany regulator clock had to go, along with everything that was not absolutely essential to life; vases, pictures, and all Mrs Brocklesby's dear little ornaments that she had collected over her lifetime. The harmonium would have gone, too, except that it was needed by Tom to practice on for that precious weekly fee that he earned at Clifton Church. Their once cosy front room began to look bleak and bare – but at least they could eat, even if their diet was limited to potatoes and vegetables for dinner and bread and lard for everything else.

Matters in many other families were far worse. Some relied entirely on wages from the pit, some were not members of the Union, and so got no strike pay. Those families pawned or sold everything, even the chairs and tables, but still could not get enough to eat. It is hard to see your treasured possessions pawned one by one, but far harder to see the pinched white faces of the children, and hear their cries for bread.

No wonder that some men swallowed their pride and slunk back to work. Though there was no coal-getting there was still work to do as the colliery company employed a few men to render the workings safe. These men were called by the derogatory nickname of 'blacklegs' (not as one local newspaper wrongly reported it, 'blackfeet', which, as Dick said, jokingly, sounded as though the colliery company had recruited a tribe of American Indians to do the work).

In keeping with their watchword, "be calm", the men had decided to let the women deal with the blacklegs. The women would wait at the roadway leading to Cadeby Colliery and greet the blacklegs with derisive shouts, the rolling of tin cans, and blowing of penny trumpets. When the schools closed for the summer holiday, the children joined these parades. It must have been humiliating to the men to run this daily gauntlet of howling women and children, for some of them responded violently. One of them was Owen Hardcastle, who had only ever thought of himself, and had no intention of going hungry when work was available. He armed himself with a pick shaft, and made to attack some of the women nearest to him. Luckily, a few men were present, and they quickly disarmed him and knocked him to the ground.

"Hit women, would, yer? Yer worm!"

"Ah'll 'ave the law on yer!"

"What, with all these witnesses to say you started it!"

"I'll get back at yer! Yer'll see!" he whimpered as he picked himself up and wiped the blood of his lips.

There were several other incidents of violence and intimidation. A man called John Hill was walking home from work one day when a man called Cairns asked him for a cigarette. When Hill replied that he didn't have one, Cairns shouted, "No, you f***ing blackleg! If you go to work on Monday I'll chuck you in t' river!"

He waited for him, too, but Hill thought the better of it and stayed at home.

As a result of an increasing number of incidents of this kind, the colliery company paid the police to protect the men who wanted to work, though the Chief Constable was reported as saying that the management were taking an unnecessary risk in bringing men into the colliery and thus provoking the strikers.

As things went from bad to worse in the village, they got better and better in church and Sunday School. When there is no other help, men turned to God, and attendance at both church and chapel increased. St Peter's choir was thriving as never before, mainly because of the penny per service paid to the choirboys. In former times this penny was seen as an incentive to get the boys to attend and face down the jeers of their friends, and parents had let them keep it to spend as they wished. Now, the 2d per Sunday was seen as a small, but valued, contribution to the squeezed family budget, and the choir stalls were packed like sardine cans with a waiting list as long as your arm.

Sunday School attendance was also at a record high, due to Gerty's idea of serving soup and bread.

"If we give them something to eat before the lessons, we will be helping their families, and they will be able to concentrate better," she had suggested to Rev Hewitt.

"That is a good idea, Gerty, and we can pay for it out of our increased collections. But I think we will serve the soup and bread after the lessons to ensure that they stay to the end."

Before or after, it was a strong incentive to attend, and numbers were so great that the church hall, large as it was, was packed. Rev Hewitt had to recruit four more volunteer teachers to teach them, and that, too, proved much easier than before, because, though the posts were voluntary, the teachers were allowed to eat as much bread and soup as they pleased.

It seemed strange indeed to Tom to walk home from this thriving concern through empty streets where groups of men hung around aimlessly, watching him with the vacant stare of cows in a field, as though wondering how anyone in Conisbrough could be walking anywhere with a sense of purpose.

But Tom was not the only one with a sense of purpose. Mr Chambers, the manager of the colliery company was determined to break the strike, and Owen Hardcastle was determined to get his revenge.

His chance came when he was approached by a representative of the colliery company at the end of his "blackleg" shift.

"I've heard that you're a man who takes no nonsense from the strikers," he began.

The man's collar and tie made Owen uneasy.

"Why, what's that to you?" he said defensively.

"I might be able to put you onto a good thing – if you've got the guts for it."

"Good thing? What do you mean?"

"I mean, how do you like the sound of £4 pound a week?"

"That's twice what I'm getting now. What do I have to do?"

"Go to court and sue the Yorkshire Miners' Association for wrongful payment of strike pay."

Owen shook his head.

"Neh, I know nowt about courts."

"You don't have to know anything about courts. The company will provide the solicitor and pay the legal fees, but they can't take action by themselves. The action must be brought by a member of the Yorkshire Miners' Association. You are a member aren't you?"

"Yeah, much good that it's done me."

"Then take the offer. The company is bound to win because the Union didn't get a two-thirds majority, so it is in breach of its own rules."

Owen thought of the daily gauntlet he had to run, and the women and children who taunted him. If they found out he was responsible for stopping their strike pay, what would they do to him then?

"Ah, can't do it, mister," he said. "It's more than me life's worth."

"The company has a nice little house in Doncaster. That's well out of the way."

Owen was tempted, but still unsure.

"Just think of it. £4 a week and nothing to do."

Owen took a deep breath. The temptation was too much for him.

"OK, I'll do it."

Can you read in history's pages of a darker deed than this? Of a wretch more than fallen, more engulfed in sin's abyss? Punishment can never be meted out to fit a crime so black; perjured, lost, debased and sunken. Time will pay this recreant back!

IV

It was November, 26 weeks since the men had come out, and attendance at Night School was at an all time low. They were now down to three: Tom, his friend, Adrian, and Mr Williams, and even they looked tired and dispirited. Mr Andrews looked the same. His usually fiery countenance was almost pale, and he preferred to sit at his desk rather than pace up and down as he did when he was on full form. It was the result of a day in a school with a rapidly dwindling school roll. Some children had left with their families who were in search of work, others were too sick or weak to attend, and those that did attend were pale and drawn.

"Eat your sandwiches, and we'll get started," he said, without enthusiasm.

He had used the money from the box, and if the truth be told, his own money as well, to buy bread for the children, which he served out each morning during registration, and also to give his adult students some energy for their two-hour lesson. But even the free bread and lard was not incentive enough for men who had begun to despair of the future. Mr Andrews was also beginning to despair. His Night School project had been going so well. It was helping the men and it was boosting his salary, now, it wasn't even helping the men – or not many of them.

"I am going to make a few changes," he announced. "As there are so few of you, and even fewer in my advanced class, I am going to amalgamate the classes. From next Tuesday there will be one session only, of one hour long. I will sit you in two groups, the general group and the advanced group, and teach each group alternately. I admit that it will not be quite the same as a full lesson, but it should be enough to keep you going until... until things get back to normal."

Tom felt depressed by this news, and he began to feel that the one chance he had to improve his life was slipping away form him.

At the end of the lesson, Mr Andrews kept Tom back for a few words. "When I decided to amalgamate my classes, I thought of your clash, Brocklesby, and chose Tuesday. This means that you can join the advanced group and make a start on arithmetic and book-keeping. If you keep it up, I'll enter you for the examination next June."

Tom's gloom was dispersed in an instant. If he could pass that examination, he could take up that offer of a job in the pit office. But then a worrying thought struck him.

Would he be considered a blackleg? No, he reassured himself. Surely by then the strikers would have achieved their victory, and everybody would be happy again.

But when he got home, there was bad news about the strike.

"The company have served ejectment orders," said Mr Brocklesby in answer to Tom's question about what the trouble was.

"What's that?" said Tom.

"Notice has been served on all miners who live in pit houses that they have to leave. Listen to this:"

Mr Brocklesby picked up a paper and began to read:

The usual course, when a landlord wants to get rid of a weekly tenant, is to serve seven day's notice, as has been done in this case. If the tenant does not give up possession of the house at the end of that time, the landlord my apply to the police court for an ejectment order, calling upon the tenant to give up possession within twenty-one days. If at the end of that period the tenant remains in the house he may be forcibly ejected.

"They can't eject us, can they dad?" said Tom.

"No. This is not a pit house, but nearly everybody in Denaby lives in a pit house. It will hit the strikers hard."

Tom thought about what his father had told him, and totting up the days and dates in his head was shocked at the conclusion.

"But that means thousands of people will be homeless at Christmas! How could the company do that? What about 'peace on earth, good will to all men?'"

"Aye, tha's got point, there, lad. If they're daft enough to put people out at Christmas there'll be such a backlash of public opinion, it could lose them the strike!"

There was indeed a backlash of public opinion as could be seen from the newspaper articles published over the next few days. One, in particular, in the form of a poem, struck

Tom as particularly powerful when it was read out in small front room at Crow Lane:

Is it fair when honest labour,
Toiling hotly, day by day
Sees the rights he fondly measures
Being slowly sapped away?
When the mighty power of Mammon,
Though it sow not, seeds to reap;
'Tis a sight to make the angel
Sadly fold her wings and weep.

And a tide of hot rebellion
Surges in the manly breast,
When he sees his home and loved ones
Baffled, cheated, and oppressed.
Could a man do less, then, think you?
With his very bread at stake,
Than to sound the note of battle
And to fight for honour's sake.

Honour to the humble miner,
Who, for six long months and more,
Silently, has fought the battle,
Hunger prowling round his door.
Only one bright ray to cheer him,
One strong rock on which to stand —
This, the golden bond of Union,
Labour's safeguard through the land.

—VERA NORMAN

Whether the company took note of the public reaction, or whether they had never intended to eject the miner's at Christmas, the ejectment order were postponed for two weeks so that the evictions would not have to take place at Christmas. It was not an act of compassion, for when the counsel for the strikers pleased for the maximum time limit of thirty days, the company insisted on the statutory twenty-one.

V

It was a few weeks after Christmas when the post came with a letter for Mr Brocklesby marked with the stamp of the Colliery Company. He tore it open, and let out a deep sigh.

"It's come," he said.

"What's come?" said Tom.

"The notice from t' company. I heard about it at t' last Union meeting, but I didn't say owt cos I didn't want to spoil Christmas."

"What does it say, dad?" said Dick.

Mr Brocklesby read the letter out loud:

DENABY AND CADEBY MAIN COLLIERIES, LIMITED

NOTICE

The ejectment orders granted by the magistrates on the 13th Dec. will be in the hands of the police to effect after the 3rd of January. All those against whom orders have been made will then be compelled to give up possession of their house.

UNLESS THEY HAVE PREVIOUSLY SIGNED THE AGREEMENT TO GO TO WORK ON THE TERMS WHEN THE PITS ARE DECLARED OPEN FOR THEM.

A final opportunity is now given of signing an agreement paper, which may be handed to the company's officer, or sent to the General Office not later than SATURDAY JAN.

3rd.

The agreement paper is as follows:-
"To the Denaby and Cadeby Main Collieries, Ltd.
I, the undersigned .... agree to
return to work when required on the same terms as existed on
the 12th July, 1902.

After the few moments it took for the contents of the letter to sink in, Dick said, "But that doesn't affect us, dad. We don't live in one of the company's houses."

"No, thank God!" said Mr Brocklesby. "I never thought ah'd be grateful for living in this damp old slum, but at least ah've got me independence!"

"Then why the doom and gloom?"

"Cos there's summat else I didna tell thee. You remember the legal action over strike pay? Well, the colliery has won, and the Yorkshire Miners' Association will pay no more strike pay after this week."

Tom was horrified. His first thought was for little Totty – this would be the death of her, surely! Mr Holdsworth's strike pay, along with that of his eldest son, could at least give her a bit of warmth and bread and lard, but without that, what would they do? Then he thought of his own family – would little Frances be next? His very soul rebelled against the idea.

"How can they do that, dad! I thought the Union supported the miners!"

Mr Brocklesby shook his head sadly.

"They've got no choice, son. If they go against t' judge's rulin', all their funds will be confiscated, and then they'll be finished."

"But what will we do?"

"We're not givin' up yet. There's another meeting tomorrow, and we'll be talking about getting' the support of the miners in other coalfields."

It seemed an uncertain prospect at best. How could the donations of other miners compare with regular strike pay? All Tom could do was follow up his plan with renewed determination.

"If there's nothing doing at Wadworth and Tickhill, I'll try Warmsworth, Balby and perhaps even Doncaster," he thought.

It was a long walk to Wadworth and Tom felt weak when he arrived at the vicarage. The story was the same, but the vicar, noticing Tom's fatigue, said he could go to the kitchen for a slice of toast and a cup of tea. There was only a housekeeper and a general maid at the vicarage, but the housekeeper was a warm-hearted old soul who took pity on Tom and gave him the best breakfast he had had for a year: as much of bacon, eggs and sausages as he could eat, washed down with a mug of strong tea made with fresh tea leaves.

Much strengthened he set out on his weary journey to Tickhill Church. That was a magnificent building, one of the largest in South Yorkshire, and he very much doubted that, even if there was a vacancy, they would consider employing a half-starved pit lad. Tom was not wrong in his estimation of his chances. He never even got to see the vicar. A message was conveyed to the clergyman by a frosty retainer, and the reply was equally frosty. The words were: "Thank you, but we have an organist already," but the tone of voice seemed to say, "and even if we hadn't we wouldn't consider employing a down-at-heel urchin like you."

Tom went back by another road which took him through Balby. There was a Roman Catholic church there, but he was politely informed that their organist worked for the glory of God and no salary was attached to the post. The vicar of Warmsworth church was equally discouraging. Tom was just beginning to think he would have to make the journey to Rawmarsh when the vicar added as an afterthought, "Have you tried Edlington?"

"I thought they had an organist?" said Tom, surprised.

"Well, Rev Harris told me that they had to manage without an organist at midnight mass. Apparently Mrs Wilkinson is getting too old for the job, and would like to retire."

Tom's heart leapt. Could this be what he was looking for? And if so, how ironic that, after tramping all these miles, he should find a job in the nearest church to Clifton! He was so excited that he refused the vicar's kind offer of a warming mug of beef tea, and set out as fast as his feet could carry him.

It was good news. Yes, they wanted an organist, and could he please start on this Sunday. The fee was 15/- per service, and there were two services every Sunday. No choir unfortunately, and very few weddings.

15/-! Tom could hardly believe it. That was as much as Mr Mews was paid at the at Conisbrough, a much larger church, but then, with the patronage of the Woodyeares, Edlington was probably just as wealthy.

"The organ is a small one," said Rev Harris, "but I am told it is a good one – a Henry Willis, I believe. Perhaps you would like to try it?"

Tom nodded, and soon they were in the church, heading down the chancel. The organ was a single manual instrument with only six stops, but the maker's label, on a brass plaque over the keyboard, showed that it was indeed a Henry Willis – one of the finest organ builders in England.

"I'll blow for you," said Rev Harris, "though I won't be able to keep it up for long."

Tom tried a few stops. Each was beautifully-voiced and was a joy to listen to, and the full organ, when all the stops were combined, was powerful without being harsh. He didn't play for long. After all, who was he, a trammer at Cadeby Colliery, that a reverend clergyman should pump the organ for him?

Tom was jubilant as he walked home through the snow.

He didn't feel the cold now. The thought of what he could do with those thirty shillings warmed him more than the thickest overcoat. But better was to come. When he broke the news to Rev Hewitt that he would no longer be able to play at Clifton, Rev Hewitt, who didn't relish the thought of taking a service without music, suggested a change to the time of morning service at Clifton so that Tom would be able to do both jobs. His weekly earnings rose to £1 17s 6d as a result of that brief conversation. He resolved immediately that he would give 15/- to Gerty for Totty, and 15/- to his mother, keeping 7/6 for emergencies. Of course, his own family must come first, and if push came to shove, he knew he would have to give it all to his mother – but hopefully, things would not get that bad. There was the Union meeting tomorrow, and the hope of funds being set from other regions.

He hurried straight round to Gawk Hole, feverish now from his exertions, and knocked on the door. Mrs Holdsworth answered. Her face was pale and strained with worry.

"How is Totty?"

"Worse."

"Take this," he said, giving her the 1/4 which was all the money he had left from last Sunday. Mrs Holdsworth gaped at the coins he had thrust into her hand with astonishment. Tom mumbled an embarrassed explanation, which included a garbled account of his new organists job, and the promise of more help. He wanted to tell the good news to Gerty, but it was another long walk to Crookhill, and anyway, he didn't like to disturb her while she was working. The strict Mrs Reynolds would not take too kindly to young men asking to see one of their maids, as the 'no followers' rule was strictly applied at Crookhill Hall. Tom smiled to himself – he wished he could really call himself that – Gerty's 'follower', or to use a nicer word, 'sweetheart'. Well, perhaps helping Totty would also help him in that direction.

IV

Tom hurried home to tell the good news to his mother, though he didn't say anything about his plan to help Gerty's family – it seemed a betrayal, somehow. Instead, he was vague about the amount he would be earning, which left him the choice of helping out in secret.

But Mrs Brocklesby was only half listening. She looked hard at Tom's red face, and felt his forehead.

"I don't like the look of you, Tom. It's a cup o' tea and straight to bed for you. All that walking around with nothin' but bread and lard in your stomach, and getting' yer feet wet in them old boots, 'as given you a fever!"

Tom protested, but his mother would hear none of it, and before long he was upstairs in bed, shivering between the sheets.

He tossed and turned all night, and was woken up by Mrs Brocklesby with a cup of weak tea.

"How do you feel this morning, love?" said his mum.

"Rotten," groaned Tom, who was aching all over. Then a thought occurred to him. "Mum, I've got to get better for tomorrow. Mrs Brocklesby shook her head. "I doubt yer'll be well enough for that. I'll send a message via Rev Hewitt."

Tom hauled himself into a sitting position.

"But I must. I must get the money. Totty will die if…"

He collapsed back onto the pillow, and his mother laid a hand on his forehead. "I'll bring you a bit o' breakfast in a minute. Just dry toast. It's all we've got – and another cup o' tea – an don't you go worryin' about Totty. Gerty's bringin' a bit o' money in. She'll be all right. It's yerself yer should be worryin' about."

Tom slept fitfully through most of the day, and was awakened by the sound of his father's heavy boots on the stairs.

"How's my lad?" said Mr Brocklesby.

"I'm all right. I've just got a cold."

Mr Brocklesby felt his forehead.

"Fever, more like. You need rest, and you need to keep warm. I'll light a fire for yer."

Tom was horrified at the waste of money.

"I'm hot enough dad. Too hot."

"Never mind. A bit of a fire will do you good. There's damp all down that wall."

Mr Brocklesby turned to go downstairs to fetch the coal, but Tom stopped him.

"What happened at the meeting, dad?"

"Don't you worry yersen about that," said Mr Brocklesby."

"I want to know. Maybe it'll put my mind at rest."

"Well, Fred Croft – you know Mr Croft – he's the chairman of the strike committee – was magnificent. He said that while the committee lived, every man was willing to stand or fall, sink or swim, live or die, to the bitter end. He said that he believed that the opposite party were playing their last trump card – a card which no other company would have played, and he cried shame on them. You should have heard the applause! He said that there had never been such a miners' struggle in Great Britain as that now in progress at Denaby and Cadeby. The good news is that the miners of Derbyshire and Yorkshire are expressing their sympathy in tangible form, and are willing to levy themselves as far as their means will allow. So there you have it, son. The strike pay from the Union may have stopped, but our fellow working men will bridge the gap."

Tom sank back on his pillow reassured that the Holdsworth family would still have a little money coming in other than Gerty's modest wages. His father made a small fire, and his mother brought up a tray of toast and tea, and what with that and the good news, he began to feel better.

"I might be able to go tomorrow, after all," he said to his mum.

"We'll see," she said, touching his forehead.

But his fever was even worse that night, and his dreams were troubled. He dreamed he felt better and went to his new organ job, but that he forgot to get dressed and arrived at the church stark naked, only to be thrown out and told he would never be allowed to darken the door of any Christian church again. Then he was stumbling back down Clifton Hill in snowstorm, still naked and shivering with cold.

His mother woke him and spooned a little soup in his mouth, after which he fell asleep again and dreamed his guardian angle was watching over him. His guardian angel had a surprising resemblance to Gerty, and when he opened his eyes, she was really there, with his sister by her side – or perhaps he dreamed the whole thing.

Another night passed and he had a vague impressions of different people coming and going. Some of them he knew, his mother, his father, his brothers, but there was a serious man whom he had seen before, but couldn't place, who tapped his chest and felt his pulse.

More strange dreams followed. He dreamed that he saw people being evicted from their houses in Denaby. There were policemen on horseback, and other policemen with cutlasses. Yet more policeman were giving a helping hand with the removals. All was calm – wasn't the watchword of the strike 'be calm'? – but there was a feeling of deep distress and a mood of pent up anger. In his dream he saw a homeless miner and his family wandering disconsolately through the streets. First came the father and mother, the latter carrying an infant in one arm and leading another just able to toddle, whilst behind them walked eight youngsters, woe-begone and miserable. It was bitterly cold, snowing, and they had nowhere to go.

He saw another large family evicted onto the street by reluctant policemen. All their goods were put outside, though they had nowhere to take them, and no means of transporting them. A policeman pointed them in the direction of a soup kitchen and they started to walk in that direction. Following them came a poor old man, whose earthly race was nearly run. The old fellow looked very weak, and seemed bewildered as he toddled along the road, coat in hand. A constable helped him to put his coat on and watched him pityingly as he toddled on his way.

The scene of his dreams shifted to the Crimea and the concentration camps where thousands of Boers and black Africans had died of starvation, disease and exposure. Then the South African Veldt somehow changed into Conisbrough Crags, and the concentration camp into a tent city for the miners and their families.

Perhaps his soul had left his body in what the 19th century Theosopher, Helena Blavatsky called 'astral projection', but such theories are scoffed at in down-to-earth Conisbrough, and it was more likely that his dreams were based on snippets of conversation that he had overheard, including a discussion of a news headline: CONCENTRATION CAMPS AT DENABY.

Whatever the source of those dreams and nightmares, the worse of all was on Wednesday night when he was at the height of his fever. In his dream, he saw the house in Gawk Hole where Gerty lived. Outside were a number of men in dark suits. They went inside, and came out again carrying a little coffin. Behind the coffin was Gerty, sobbing her heart out, and behind her the rest of her family in a similar heartbroken state.

Tom woke up suddenly shouting: "No! No!"

His mother came rushing up stairs.

"What is it, Tom?"

"It's Totty!" sobbed Tom. "She's dead!"

"Well, that's the first I've heard of it, Tom, love," said Mrs Brocklesby, trying to calm him down.

"She is! I saw her little coffin!"

"It was just a bad dream," said his mother, comfortingly.

"Perhaps it really happened. Send Harry to find out."

Mrs Brocklesby shook her head with disbelief. "Well if it's the only way to get you to calm down, I will. Harry!" she shouted.

"What, mam?"

"Go round to t' Holdsworth's and check that everythin's all right. Dick!"

"What, mam?"

"Mek a cuppa tea for our Tom. Use them fresh leaves an' mek it strong. He needs a bit of a pick up!"

Tom sat up in bed and drank his tea with hands that trembled as he held the cup. Even as he drank, the horror of the nightmare began to fade – but its message didn't.

"Mum, I wanted to help Totty with my organist's pay, but then I fell sick. I feel so useless!"

"Don't be silly, love. You've done a lot to help everybody."

Just then, Harry got back, and shouted up the stairs.

"They're all reet!"

"What about Totty?" Jack called, or tried to call, but he only made a kind of croak. Harry got the message however.

"Her an' all!"

"Is she getting better?"

"No, but she's no worse."

Tom breathed a sigh of relief, then looked earnestly at his mother.

"Mum, I want you to do something for me."

"What is it, love?"

"Sell my harmonium and give the money to Mrs Holdsworth for food for Totty."

"Not your harmonium! We've hung on to that through thick and thin because your organ playin' is all that's keepin' us – that, and Alice's bit from t' Old Hall."

"I can get another one when times are better, but…"

"Yes, I know what you mean. I'll get yer dad to see to it."

The whole family asked around, and in the end it was Alice who sold it by mentioning it to Mr Allport. Mrs Allport was tired of her plonky old upright piano and had been thinking of changing it for an organ for some time. In its renovated state it was worth at least 30/-, and Mr Allport, impressed by its gleaming casework and mellow tone, and mindful of the hardship that had brought about its sale, gave them £2 for it. Tom requested that the £2 go straight to the Holdsworths, and that they buy every manner of good thing to build up Totty's strength: soup, beef tea, grapes, bananas – anything and everything that could be found in Conisbrough that might do Totty good.

By Wednesday, Tom was well enough to come downstairs, and was surprised to see the small front room heaving with people.

"Hey up, Tom, lad."

It was Joe, his uncle.

"Joe's stayin' wi' us until t' strike's over," explained dad. "So we'll be a bit cramped. I'm going to put 'em in t' back bedroom, so tha'll 'ave ter sleep on t' floor wi' us."

"Are tha all reet?" said Ted, his cousin, a boy of about the same age.

"Aye," said Tom. "Just a bit wobbly on my legs after laying on my back for God knows how long."

"There's a pot o' tea brewin' an' there's some bread an' lard on t' table," said Mrs Brocklesby. "Tuck in, now, afore it gets eaten up. You need to build yer strength up."

"Any news of Totty, mum?" said Tom, his cheeks bulging with bread and lard.

"Aye, she's doin' well now. Thanks to thee."

Tom was delighted to hear the news, and thought about going round to see her.

"But it's a pity about your harmonium. How are you goin' to manage without it, new organ job an' all?"

"Don't worry mum. I'll go to church this after and practice on their harmonium – an' I'll pop in and see Totty on the way."

"Nay, lad. Tha's only just come downstairs. Stay in today. Tomorrow's soon enough to be trampin' round t' village in the freezin' cold."

"All right, mum. I'll leave it till tomorrow. I can go an hour early to choir practice and get my hand in again before Sunday. In the meantime I can practice in the air like I did when I was a trapper."

His mum gave him a puzzled look, and Tom demonstrated by playing on an imaginary keyboard.

At first, it was fun to have his cousins living with him, but the novelty soon wore off, and everybody seemed to be in everybody else's way. Still, they were not the only family living like that. Half the households in Conisbrough were giving shelter to Denaby friends or relatives, but there were still hundred of families who had to live in tents, despite the freezing cold.

VII

Sunday was a big day for Tom. He arrived at Edlington Church very early so that he would have time to sort out his music, and arrange for a boy to pump the organ. Rev Morris was delighted to see him. He had persuaded Mrs Wilkinson to come out of retirement for the last two Sundays, but she had made it clear that she couldn't continue to play with a gale blowing through her fingers. When Tom sat down at the keyboard he found out what she meant. The organ had been built into an arch which separated the vestry from the chancel, and every time the vestry door opened, a chilly draught would go straight through the instrument and up through the gaps between the keys. It was so bad, that Tom made a mental note to bring his fingerless gloves next Sunday. Edlington Church had not benefited from the renovation that had given Conisbrough Church pipes and a boiler.

He felt that he played well, the rich tones of the Father Willis pipework inspiring him to give of his best. For the last verse of the last hymn he pulled out all six stops and played an octave higher with his right hand to give extra brilliance. The small congregation responded with their heartiest singing. It was very satisfying.

After the service the church warden complimented Tom on his playing, and for using all the stops.

"Old Mrs Wilkinson was a pianist really, an' she had the same two stops out for twenty years. I didn't know t' old organ could sound so grand!"

But Tom had no time to linger. He had to get over to Clifton for 10.00, and it was a good mile's walk. Rev Hewitt was pleased to see him as they had had no music at all for the past two Sundays, and Tom was pleased to settle down in his old berth at the two manual harmonium.

Then it was back to Conisbrough with money jingling in his pocket. His first stop was Gawk Hole, where he gave 10/- to Mrs Brocklesby, then he hurried home to give the rest to his mother so that she could go out and buy something for Sunday dinner.

"Oh, Tom," she said, "I feel bad about takin' yer money. What about you?"

"I'll get more this evening," said Tom with the nonchalance of a rich manufacturer.

There were so many at Crow Lane, and so little in the way of crockery, that dinner had to be served in shifts. Grandpa and three youngest children sat in the only four chairs they had left, and everybody else sat where they could. They had potatoes, vegetables and a small piece of scrag end of neck, the only meat they would taste until next Sunday dinner. This was followed by tea made with fresh tea leaves, and served in a variety of receptacles from the few remaining cups, to jam jars. Tom relished the taste of the strong brown liquid, though he missed the milk that softened it, and the sugar that sweetened it. Milk and sugar were impossible luxuries just then, but at least the tea was fresh. The leaves would be re-used again and again, and the brew would taste weaker and weaker until it was little better than warm water. The fire, too, was bigger and warmer than usual, but what warmed Tom the most was the thought of seeing Gerty that afternoon.

At Sunday School it was difficult to speak freely with the Rev Hewitt looking on, but everything that Tom had hoped to see was in Gerty's eyes. She give him a warm, shy look that said it all; her thanks for what he had done for Totty, and her increased regard for him as a person. When the lessons were over, and the three of them, Alice, Gerty and Tom, were walking towards Crow Lane, she was able to put her thanks into words.

"I don't know what would have happened without you, Tom. You saved our Totty's life."

"Well, I don't know about that," said Tom, blushing. "Maybe I helped a bit."

"You did," said Gerty, "and I can see what it cost you."

She was looking at his boots. They were his best pair, but they were still worn down to nothing.

"When this strike's over…" he began.

"Oh I'm sick o' the strike!" she said. "All this suffering – and what has it got us?"

But Tom had no answer. Walking beside Gerty, basking in her heartfelt thanks, was seventh heaven to Tom, and at that moment he was the last person in the world to be able to empathise with suffering humanity.

It was not long before they reached Crow Lane.

"I'll not ask you in, Gerty," said Alice. "My uncle's stayin' an it'll be choc-a bloc in there."

"What, not ask Gerty in?" said Tom, aghast.

"It's all right Tom," said Gerty. "I understand. It's the same at our house. Ta ta."

And with that, she began to walk away. But Tom had something else to say. He had hoped to lead in to it naturally at the end of the afternoon, but now he had no choice but to blurt it out.

"Will you walk up wi' me?"

Gerty turned round, surprised.

"I've got a new job at Edlington Church and I'll be walking up for evensong at six."

"Oh, that'll be nice," replied Gerty, as though it was nothing more than a common sense arrangement between two friends who happened to be going in the same direction. However, Tom was happy enough, and he had to bite his lips to stop himself smiling and giving his secret away to his sister.

On Tuesday he went to Night School, but was disappointed to find that the windows of Morley Place School were dark and the door was locked. Next morning, he was up early to catch Mr Andrews before school started.

"I've stopped the classes until further notice," he explained. "There were so few coming that it hardly seemed worth the effort."

Tom's heart sank. All his hopes were founded on the Night School and the examination that would get him out of the pit. He had not handled a shovel for 30 odd weeks, and his hands had regained their old softness and suppleness, and despite his poor diet, the fresh air and daylight had given him a healthier complexion. His disappointment must have been obvious, because Mr Andrews added, "when the strike's over, I'm sure things will get back to normal."

"But the examination's in May," said Tom. "That's only two months and a bit, and there's so much to do."

"Well, you could postpone the examination until next year. In any case, there is an examination fee to be paid, and I don't suppose you can get the money, things being what they are."

Tom thought of his earnings from organ playing – and

then of the many calls on them.

"How much?" He hardly dared to ask the question.

"That's just it," said Mr Andrews. "It's 30/-. That's a lot at the best of times."

Tom did a quick calculation. It was less than one Sunday's earnings, and it was certain that there would be one or two weddings or funeral between now and then. He could do it! He explained about his new organ job to Mr Andrews, but his enthusiasm wavered as he came back to the problem: "…but without a teacher…"

Mr Andrews heaved a deep sigh.

"I'll be frank with you, Tom. You know my enthusiasm for learning; my belief that it can change lives for the better? Well, that's taken a bit of a knock, recently. What happened to all those men who came to my classes? What future have they now? And look at me. I struggled and strived to escape from the Cotton Mills where my family worked. I went to Night School like you. I studied hard. I went to college – but where did it get me? An elementary school, teaching the alphabet and money sums, and a salary that's less than a hewer's."

"But it's a good job," Mr Andrews, protested Tom, "it's a job that people respect. You help people. You give them a chance – the only chance they'll ever get in a place like this!"

Mr Andrews shook his head. "I'm not sure, Tom. I'm not sure anymore. It's this strike. It's getting us all down. Perhaps you think I'm not affected, but look – this is what I have to face every day."

His class were beginning to assemble. They were shabbily dressed, many were barefoot, their faces were pasty, and they seemed to have no energy.

"And look at this…"

He showed Tom the register. Flicking through the pages he showed how the school roll had declined since the strike began. "Some families have moved away. Other children are too sick to come, others just don't see the point of anything."

He looked around, and deciding that the class was as complete as it was going to be, summoned two monitors to give out the bread.

"I give them a crust of bread for breakfast in the hope of giving them a bit of energy for learning – but it's not bread they need, it's meat – a healthy diet, and hope. It's much worse in Denaby, I'm told."

Tom surveyed the sorry scene and realized that it would be selfish to press for help with his own aspirations.

"I understand," he said with a sigh.

But Mr Andrews guessed what he was thinking, and seemed to come to a decision.

"In all this – mess – you are the only hope. You are my best student, and Adrian is not far behind. If you could pass that examination you could make something of your life, and be the living proof that my old belief was not a hollow cheat after all. Yes. Come next Tuesday and we'll carry on. Tell Adrian to come too."

VIII

When Tom got back to Crow Lane, a heated discussion was in progress.

"What's up, dad," said Tom.

"The collieries have reopened for work and they're bringing in new labour from other areas ,"

"Aye, and we're going to stop 'em!" cried Uncle Joe.

"How?"

"We're going to organize a procession to demonstrate against them, and we're going to picket the colliery gates. We're passing the word today, and we'll be there this afternoon to deal wi' them blacklegs. Yer dad's helping to organize it."

"Will it work, dad?" asked Tom.

Tom saw from the expression in his father's face that he very much doubted it. He had worn the same defeated look since before Christmas, for he knew full well that without strike funds the strike would fail. He also knew that, after suffering so much, the men wouldn't give in without a fight, so as one of their appointed leaders, he had to fight on.

"If we can see them blacklegs off, it might," he said.

"Can I come?" said Tom.

"Aye, lad, but keep well back in case there's any trouble."

It seemed that every striking miner was on the march that day. There were over two thousand men and almost as many women. They marched from the Conisbrough Lodge rooms at the Station Hotel towards the two collieries, and met a party of workers marching returning from the pits, and in a moment the air was filled with excitement, yells and insults being flung at the coal-begrimed colliery hands, who were immediately surrounded by mounted police. When this demonstration was at its height, a blinding snow storm swept full in the teeth of the crowd, who took but little notice of it, and pressed forward, the women even forgetting the exposure to which they were subjecting their infants. As the procession continued, the workers slipped away one by one, some to their homes in Denaby or Conisbrough, and most of them to places of safety further away.

Several men were charged as a result of that day's proceedings. Charges such as 'watching and besetting', 'conspiraciy to intimidate' and 'disorderly behaviour' were brought by a few of the workers, who were, no doubt, encouraged and supported by the company.

This went on every day, apart from the blissful interval of Sunday, when Tom seemed to enter that other, enchanted world of Romance. He was not as forward as his brother, and was careful to keep his conversation general on that long, slow walk up to Crookhill Hall. Gerty asked him about the blacklegs, and he told her everything that had happened. She shook her head sadly as she listened, for though she had little knowledge of the ins-and-outs of the affair, she had a woman's instinct that all the suffering her family had endured was for nothing.

On Tuesday, Tom resumed his lessons with Mr Andrews who seemed filled with renewed purpose. He now had a specific goal – to get Tom through the May examination. Adrian was preparing for it too, but unless the strike ended soon, it was unlikely that he would be able to afford the entrance fee.

The processions and picketing continued, along with numerous Union meetings, and it was after one of these that Mr Brocklesby came home with the blackest expression that Tom had ever seen.

"It's over," he said.

Nobody need to ask the question, "who won?" because the answer could be seen in Mr Brocklesby's face.

"What happened?" said Uncle Joe.

"The Executive Council of the Miners' Federation have advised the men to return to work on t' old terms. They took legal advice, o' course. You see, the Union is in danger o' being sued by the company and losin' all its funds."

"Because they didn't get the two-thirds majority?"

"Aye, I allus said they was too hasty in coming out. If only they'd 've waited until they got that majority. But it's too late now. I've just come from a meeting of the Yorkshire Miners' Association, and they are recommending that the men resume work."

"But we can still fight on!" said Uncle Joe, unable to accept it.

"Aye," said Dick, and then quoting something he had heart Mr Croft say in one of his stirring speeches, "True till death or victory!"

Mr Brocklesby shook his head.

"It's no good. Don't yer see that, now that the Union itself has advised us to return to work that those – blacklegs – are not blacklegs any longer. They're not strike breakers, because, from today, there is no strike – well, not officially!"

"Well. I agree with Croft," said Uncle Joe.

"Me, too," said Dick.

"We've suffered too much to give in now."

But Mr Brocklesby seemed not to hear them. He had more bad news to tell.

"The company will take any of the old workers back on the old terms, but first priority will be given to those that signed the paper – and there are new men now."

"The blacklegs!" cried Uncle Joe.

"Call them what you like, but I fear that the men who have been most loyal to the strike will suffer the most... and the delegates most of all."

Tom looked alarmed.

"What do you mean, dad?"

"I mean that any man who is seen as being a leader in the strike will never be employed by the company again."

Mr Brocklesby slumped down on the only unoccupied chair.

"A good man like you is sure to get work somewhere else," said Mrs Brocklesby.

"Nay, lass. We'll be painted as trouble makers, and no employer will touch us."

"Dunna thee worry thysen," said Uncle Joe with a gruffer kind of comfort. "We'll fight the good fight till death or victory!"

So the angry processions and the pickets carried on, though every day the numbers in the processions were smaller and the number of workers was larger. By April, the colliery was almost back to full output, but there were still over a thousand men unemployed and living in tents.

Mr Holdsworth had managed to get his job back, so things were almost back to normal in his household. Dick was still out of work. Possibly the Brocklesby name had something to do with it, as it was associated in the minds of the company with one of the Union delegates, so matters in the Brocklesby household continued much as before.

Tom did not even try to get his old job back. His earnings as an organist were enough to keep him going, and he had an eye on that clerk's stool in the pit offices, though he realized that there was a black cloud looming on that horizon.

"Will the Brocklesby name go against me, do you think?" he asked Mr Andrews after one of their lessons.

Mr Andrews laughed. "I shouldn't worry about that. There are plenty of counting houses would jump at the chance of a young man with a qualification like yours."

"I haven't got it yet."

"Then stop worrying and start working!"

EPILOGUE

In May, Tom passed his Book-keeping examination with honours, and Mr Jameson was as good as his word, though it took a bit of persuasion from himself and a reference from Mr Andrews to overcome the prejudice against the Brocklesby name. It was this comment by Mr Jameson that swung it: "Well, he's a promising young man, and if you don't want him there's plenty of others that will."

So by July, Tom was seated on that much-coveted counting house stool. The work was duller than he expected. He had to work through a pile of invoices, enter them in a ledger and tot up the figures so that the debit and credit columns tallied. There was no call at all for the fancy formulas that he had had to learn for the examination. It was just simple arithmetic which he could have done on the day he left school. But then he remembered Mr Andrews. He had studied for his teacher's certificate, and no doubt felt that his knowledge was of little use when it came to teaching in an elementary school. Tom was also disappointed with the pay. It was less than a hewer might earn at piece work, but it was a salary, not a wage. He was paid monthly, and was paid during public holidays, and if he had a day off sick. He was also accumulating a modest pension. The main thing for Tom, however, was that it was clean, and that, apart from ink-stains, his hands did not suffer. Also, he wore a suit for work, and white starched collars and cuffs. He felt that he was another class of being to the person he was when he had worked as a trammer — not that he was the kind who would look down on the working man — hadn't he been one of them? — wasn't his family a collier's family and proud of it? No, he valued it because he felt if made him worthier of his sweetheart. He had achieved something in life — not much, perhaps, but then, his life was only just beginning — and he felt that achievement made him a worthy prospect as a husband. Though it would be a long time yet before he would be old enough, or wealthy enough, to take that step.

His main worry at that time was his father. Mr Brocklesby had always prided himself on what he called his work ethic. He had worked for his family as a miner, and he had worked to better the lot of the miners through the Union, but he had lost both of them through the recent strike. He was saved through what a Christian might call the intervention of Providence, or Buddhist might call Karma. Whatever name you want to give it, it was a good deed of his, followed by a good deed of Tom's, that bore fruit a hundredfold.

Mrs Allport was delighted with her new harmonium, and when she heard how it had been renovated from a dusty ruin, she asked her husband to enquire if the same magic might be worked on an old Jacobean sideboard which had laid for many year in the attic.

Mr Brocklesby promised to do his best, and the first

step was to re-equip his workshop with a few basic tools – all his old tools having been sold off during the strike. He saw at once that the sideboard had been well made out of good materials by craftsmen who loved their work, though it had been sadly neglected. A carved baluster was missing from the top and a door was missing from the front. At some point it had been used as a workbench, and the top was badly scored and dented. Mr Brockelesby set up his old lathe – it had not been sold because it was a simple home-made affair and worth nothing – and turned a baluster out of a piece of battered old oak he picked up at the woodyard for a few coppers. Then he set to work with his chisels and gouges to reproduce the delicate fluting. He replaced the door with another piece of oak, and spent hours on the delicate carved mouldings that framed it. He smoothed down the top with a home-made scraper, a box-plane being more than Tom could afford to buy him just then. The hardest job was toning the new oak, almost white from the shaping and scraping, to match the dark old oak, and he did this with a home made stain consisting mainly of old tea leaves. The final touch was the finish – not varnish, oh no! nothing as brash and modern as varnish out of a tin. Instead, he used his own mixture of shellac and turpentine with a dash of linseed oil and splash from the vinegar bottle borrowed from the kitchen, and he rubbed it in with a cloth and much elbow grease. The result was a sheen that seemed to emanate from the wood itself, rather than a surface gloss that had been painted on. It was a labour of love. Work for the love of the work, as Marx had urged, and he was sorry when it was finished. Mrs Allport was thrilled with the end product.

"Why it looks as good as new – and somehow, still centuries old. It's wonderful. Mr Brocklesby, you should go into business restoring and making furniture."

"I've no head for business, ma'am," he said, modestly.

"Oh, you don't need that. This is not counting-house

work! You need what you've got – what shall I call it? – a magic touch! I shall put the word around my friends, and I'm sure you'll get plenty of work."

And he did. So much so that he asked Dick to work with him, and soon they were making more money together than they had ever done down the pit.

Providence had another consequence to work out. Owen Hardcastle had lived very well for the past 10 months on the four pounds a week that the colliery paid him. He had good lodgings in Doncaster and no work to do. He took life easily, attending the races when they were on, and hanging around disreputable taverns when they were not. He thought he was made for life, and was on the look out for some promising little woman to share it with him, when the rude awakening came. He received a letter one day informing him that the colliery had no further need of his services, and that the payments would stop with effect from the following Saturday. He was at his wits end. What could he do? He would not dare to show his face anywhere in Conisbrough or Denaby, and the employers of Doncaster did not want to know him, as he had the reputation of being 'a bad lot'. Rumour had it that he took a train to Nottingham and tried his luck there, but never succeeded in holding a job down, and ended up as one of those ragged individuals who beg their way from town to town and sleep under hedgerows.

8. CONISBROUGH RAILWAY TRAIL

Conisbrough Viaduct is at least as impressive as Conisbough Castle though it receives much less attention. It was opened on March 17, 1909 and closed in 1966. In 2001 its ownership was transferred to Railway Paths Ltd and it was linked to the Trans Pennine Trail at its north-western end. This anecdote from the 1960's describes me and my friends exploring the railway long before it became an official Railway Trail.

At the top of Clifton Hill, just after the junction to Clifton, there is short wall made of dark blue-grey engineering brick with a pillar at each end. It looks like a railway bridge, but if you look over the parapet, there is nothing below, just a level field. Many years ago there was a railway cutting there.

As children, we often walked over the bridge, on the way to Edlington Woods, or Conisbrough Parks, and, being children, we would lean over the bridge parapet and look at the railway below. Sometimes we would wait to see a train, but we never saw one.

One day we noticed that a train of wagons had been

shunted there. The wagons looked empty, and rather rusty and dilapidated. It was as though they had been put there out of the way. When they were still there, several months later, we decided that they had been forgotten about and that it would be safe to take a look.

So me and my mates Stephen and Finlay, with his little Scottie dog, ventured down the embankment to the railway line. The brown rust on top of the rails told its story. This line was hardly ever used. Now that we felt certain that we were unlikely to be run over or carried away, we climbed into one of the wagons. In the bottom were thousands of tine steel disks, about the size of a sixpence, but much thicker. What they were for we couldn't imagine, but they were clearly the remnants of some industrial freight.

After spending a while in the wagons we decided to follow the line east. We jumped from sleeper to sleeper, or balanced on the rails, while batting at the luxuriant undergrowth that was beginning to invade the track. The undergrowth was reassuring, for it was yet more evidence that the line was disused.

After a few miles we came to a junction. We could see at once that the other line was very much in use as the tops of the rails gleamed brilliantly in the sun. We had no sooner observed this when a Black Five, chuffing valiantly at the head of a long train of coal wagons, appeared round a distant bend. We retreated at once, not wanting to get into trouble, and made our way back down the line to the cutting and the bridge.

On our next venture we went east towards Doncaster. After a few miles we came to another junction, but this time the other line looked as disused as the one we had followed, so we decided to carry on.

After a while, we came to the head of Conisbrough Viaduct. The view in both directions was magnificient – probably the best view in Conisbrough – even better than the view from the top of the castle. The valley of the Don, though marred by Cadeby Colliery and Conisbrough Station to the west, was as wild as it was in ancient times if you looked towards Doncaster. To the north were Cadeby Cliffs, topped by woodland, and in the valley was luxuriant green undergrowth going right down to the edges of the gleaming River Don.

We were afraid to cross the viaduct, not because we feared it would fall down, though it did look neglected, but because we were afraid somebody might see us and that we would get into trouble – we worried about such things in those days! In the end, we ventured out about 20 paces before our nerve failed, and we ran back.

Having explored the line in both directions as far as we dared, we lost interest in it in favour of the so-called 'haunted' houses in Clifton. Today Clifton is a wealthy suburb of Conisbrough, but in those days, many of the houses had fallen into semi-ruin.

A year or so later, we were crossing the bridge when we noticed that the wagons had gone. This piqued our interest enough to descend into the cutting again and follow the line in a westerly direction. How things had changed! Not only had the wagons gone, but the track had been lifted. We only got a few hundred yards because landowners had started to encroach upon the railway track. It was the same in the other direction.

It was many years later that I noticed that the cutting had been filled in, and, apart from the bridge parapet there was no sign that the railway had ever been there. I couldn't help wondering why it had ever been thought worth the expense of building such an enormous viaduct if it was possible to do without it a mere 55 years later.

I have not yet crossed the viaduct on the official railway trail and I am looking forward to the prospect, When I do, I will no doubt remember vividly my first outing on the unofficial 'Railway Trail' over half a century ago.

ABOUT THE AUTHOR

Christopher Webster was brought up in Conisbrough, went to Station Road School, and has lived at various times on Daylands Avenue, Roberts Avenue and Castle Avenue. The town, with its rich history and magnificent castle, has been an important influence in his life, and has inspired some of his best work. He read English at St David's, Lampeter, and Leeds University, and has taught English in several countries, including Germany, Bermuda, Belgium and Singapore. His first educational publication was *Poetry Through Humour and Horror* (Cassell, 1987). This was followed by many more, including books for KS3 and GCSE English Language and Literature published by Hodder, and the best-selling *100 Literacy Hours* (Scholastic, 1997/2005). He has also written several novels, including novels about Conisbrough history, most recently, *The Abduction of Lady Alice*, and a collection of narrative poems called *Conisbrough Tales*, which he describes as a *Canturbury Tales* for Conisbrough.